BONSATILUM: RIDIFICCI

Good Enough Evil Collection #1

Regis Floats

CONTENTS

Title Page
Volume 1   1
 Passage #1: The Unforeseen Wish   3
Passage #2: Superpowered Bar Fight   5
Passage #3: The Hunt is Over   7
Passage #4: The Elemental   10
Passage #5: The Finest Security System   13
Passage #6: A Special Morning   16
Passage #7: The Superhero and The Citizen   18
Passage #8: The Ridificci Lifestyle   21
Passage #9: The Heiress and The Citizen   24
Passage #10: A Time to Fight   27
Volume 2   33
Passage #1: "Wind Affinity: Space" Day   34
Passage #2: Golden Opportunity   36
 Passage #3: On-the-Sideshow Career   40
Passage #4: The Vagabond vs. The Citizen   42

Passage #5: A Time to Talk	50
Passage #6: Just a Nightmare	55
Passage #7: The Tour	57
Passage #8: Wapaloosie Walking	62
Passage #9: Tales of the Ivory Roamer- Part 1	65
Passage #10: Important Messages	68
Volume 3	71
Passage #1: Infiltration	72
Passage #2: Destiny's Dark Champion	75
Passage #3: The Proposition	79
Passage #4: The Chosen One vs. The Citizen - Rematch	81
Passage #5: The Big Talk	86
Passage #6: "Jānī Obu Jānī: Atarashi jidai" Episode 1	90
Passage #7: Team Trip- Day 2	93
Passage #8: Team Trip- Night 5	96
Passage #9: The Final Day of The Trip	100
Passage #10: Pranks at the Pews	104
Volume 4	107
Passage #1: Intelligence Meeting	108
Passage #2: Just a Dream	116
Passage #3: The Explorer and The Revived Kingdom of Illecelucuu	119
Passage #4: The Chosen One & The Mutant VS	124

The Field Marshal & The Citizen

Passage #5: A Visit from THE MERITORIOUS KNIGHT	131
Passage #6: The Dark One's Dark Secret	136
Passage #7: Music-Making	140
Passage #8: Redesign	143
Passage# 9: Let's Talk about You	146
Passage# 10: The Expedition (Part 1)	149
Volume 5	153
Passage #1: The Expedition (Part 2)	154
Passage #2: Tales of The Ivory Roamer- Part 4	160
Passage #3: The Chosen One's Crew	164
Passage #4: The Prologue of The Destined Battle	168
Passage #5: The Destined Battle: Change is Coming	173
Passage #6: The Destined Battle: Change is Here	179
Passage #7: The Destined Battle: Change is Here to Stay	183
Passage #8: Epilogue of The Destined Battle	189
Passage #9: An Awkward Chat	192
Passage #10: A Stroll Around Town	196
Acknowledgement	201
Contact	203

VOLUME 1

Published October 22, 2018

PASSAGE #1: THE UNFORESEEN WISH

In an ancient tomb far below the surface of a desert, a teenage boy stood in front of a sentient, green orb that grants any wish by twisting the very physical plane of reality. Behind him was an adventurer who wished for the Midas Touch on his left hand, but the rest of him was turned to gold. A scientist, who was also with them, lay dead because he wished to know the true meaning of life. His last words were "Literature," "Entertainment," and "Pointless Character." His mind could not cope with the knowledge that he had learned.

With an enticing feminine tone, The Orb said, "What is your wish, young master."

The Teenager just stood there thinking of the many possible wishes that could backfire on him. After several minutes of intense thinking, the boy finally decided what he wanted.

On his knees, he exclaimed, "Orb, I wish for you to teach me the things that you can do! I want you to be my master?"

Not seeing wish coming, The Orb said, "What? Why would you wish for that?"

The Teenager said, "I read many stories on things

that grant wishes like genies and the monkey's paw. I always thought that those things that grant wishes too literally were simply evil, but now I realize that it is because you are slaves. The only way you could have some freedom is to punish your masters through their wishes. I don't want to get something the easy way. I wish to earn it."

"I never met a human like you before," The Orb said. "I will grant your wish and teach you to craft your supernatural gift."

The Orb opened a portal that leads into its world. The portal swirls like a whirlpool with many shooting stars trapped within it.

"Come into my world, my pupil. Your training awaits you," said The Orb.

"Yes, Master." The Teenager said as he walked through the portal.

PASSAGE #2: SUPERPOWERED BAR FIGHT

At night, in a tavern, a citizen decided to go back to his apartment to go to bed after he ate his last French Fry. Before moving from his seat, four men with guns came into the bar. A man with a fedora followed them in and carried an oddly large suitcase.

"Everyone, drop all your valuables and don't do anything else." The Thug Leader said. "There's no point in resisting. We got all the power here."

The Citizen sighed and thought about doing something. Then a humanlike figure came out of nowhere in a bright cyan blue outfit and visor. He jumped right in front of the thugs, radiating a glow of intense earth-shaking power. Everyone recognized him as that superhero from the news. The thugs tried to shoot him, but the bullets just stopped within his bright aura. The Superhero knocked them out with a powerful energy wave. Still standing, The Thug Leader pulled out a high-tech gun from his suitcase.

"Stay back, you **************!" he screamed. "This gun is designed to kill an elephant in one shot, and just imagine what would happen to all these innocent people."

The Thug Leader turned his head, saw a woman

on the ground using her cellphone, and then looked back at his enemy. The Superhero moved forward to get him, but The Thug Leader pointed his gun toward the bystanders.

As The Thug Leader cocked his gun, He said, "Since someone has already called the cops, I'll just shoot now."

The Citizen pulled back his fist towards the Thug Leader. He thrust (Strength: Space) his fist forward, and The Thug Leader was pushed back by an unknown force dropping his gun in the process. Before The Thug Leader could rationalize what just happened, The Superhero punched him in the jaw knocking him out. The people cheered for The Superhero for saving their lives, and The Citizen left the bar unnoticed.

PASSAGE #3: THE HUNT IS OVER

A chase between a man and something supernatural had already begun at an apartment building. The Citizen recently bought a coat made from Wapoloosie pelts from an auction of mysterious items. As soon as he puts it down, it climbed up to the ceiling and fled out The Citizen's front door of his apartment. Just then, a mysterious woman in a black jacket with war paint on her face attacked him from behind because she was after his coat as well. The two went out and found the target down a hallway, and they ran towards it with high velocity.

The Citizen yelled, "You're not going to have my coat you... you... Intruder!"

The Intruder said, "Look, I need it. My tribe needs it, and you can have it back when we're done with it."

The Citizen started to slow down because he was a bit out of shape. Several feet away, The Intruder reached for the coat that was moving across the ceiling. The Citizen (Speed: Time) ran as time slowed down, and he caught up with her as she grabbed the jacket. The two pulled the coat like two children who cannot share one toy. Then one of the seams of the coat ripped open, and a coin popped out. The Intruder let go of the jacket and reached for it, and The Citizen quickly grabbed the gold piece before she could get it.

The Intruder yelled, "Give that to me! That is what I want!"

The Citizen asked, "Why do you need some old coin?"

The Intruder said with tears in her eyes, "Because it is worth a lot to my tribe. It's worth a lot of money. My tribe was going to sell it to save our home, but an evil skin-walker stole it. He died before selling it, but he hid it in one of his coats. I looked through every single one of those coats, and I am not going to leave now empty-handed!"

Before The Intruder could reach for the knife hidden in her black jacket, The Citizen tossed the coin to her. The Intruder grabbed the medal and stared at The Citizen.

The Intruder said, "Why are you giving this to me?"

The Citizen said, "First of all, I just wanted my coat. It's comfortable, and it is special. It is like a pet that I don't have to feed or bathe. It might look ridiculous when I wear it, but I don't care. The other reason is that I like to earn my fortune rather than take it from another, especially since you need it more than I do. Now, go and save your tribe."

As she walked to an open elevator, The Intruder winked and said, "Thank you." The elevator door closed, and The Citizen walked to his room. He checked the ripped seam to see if it was severe and sighed because he knew he could sew it back. He let the coat run freely around the wall and ceilings with the door and windows closed shut.

The Citizen said to the coat, "Well, Meredith, I managed to keep you and made one other person happy. Even if she may have made up that story, I am just happy to have you, but I could really use that kind of money right about now."

PASSAGE #4: THE ELEMENTAL

The Citizen and his friend, a geologist, walked toward an entrance blocked by rocks in a cave. He called The Citizen to help him with a peculiar expedition that required his unique skills and experience.

The Geologist said, "It is time for the task at hand. I need you to distract an earth elemental, a creature made from various rocks and ores, while I go get the mineral that it is guarding."

With a hint of concern, The Citizen said, "Okay, but why couldn't you call the military to do this if there is only one?"

The Geologist answered, "I did, and it already killed three squads."

The Citizen said, "I see. It looks like I am the only one who can do this. So, where is it?"

The Geologist replied, "It is behind that wall of boulders that I covered with C4."

The Citizen said, "Great. Well, open the door."

"Roger, opening up the doorway in...." The Geologist said as he stood at a safe distance from the impending explosion, "...5...4... 3...2...1... 0."

All the explosives went off and cleared the path. The Citizen ran in, ready to face the creature. He jumped through the threshold, all pumped up with adrenaline, but the elemental was already dead. Its body scattered around a rocky bridge suspended above a pool of lava.

The Citizen said, "Ah, dude?"

The Geologist responded, "Yes?"

The Citizen said, "The monster is dead."

The Geologist said, "You beat it already?"

The Citizen said, "No, it probably died when you blew up the wall."

The Geologist said, "Oh, okay."

The two men mined for the rare minerals on the other side of the bridge and put them in crates. The Citizen grabbed the last container, and both men moved toward the threshold.

"I did not foresee this turn of events." The Geologist said, "I killed a monster that killed three highly trained squads."

The Citizen said, "Life has its ways of turning you into the hero of the story."

The elemental put itself together and roared right behind them as they stood within the threshold. Both men screamed and ran with only two crates.

The Geologist pressed a button on his jacket and

shrieked, "Keep Running!"

"I am running!" The Citizen shouted, "Why do I need to run even more?"

The Geologist yelled, "Because I activated the self-destruct sequence!"

The Citizen bellowed, "Okay, then hold on to me!"

The Geologist grabbed him. The Citizen took (Agility: Probability) one step, and a piece of earth rose to launch them. Then another rock appeared, and he jumped on that one. Then more rocks appeared, and he bounced on all of them to further themselves from the creature. They both made it to the surface of the mountainous terrain as the cave went up in flames, but they both kept on running and screaming. They were too scared of stopping to see if their pursuer was still chasing behind them. It did survive one explosion, and it might have survived the second one.

PASSAGE #5: THE FINEST SECURITY SYSTEM

A thief had infiltrated a government storage facility and beat all the facility's securities, traps, and even a robot. The Citizen watched all the events through his monitors. As The Thief was running down the hallway, a speaker announced, "Mr. Thief, this is the manager speaking. Please, come to my office on the third floor."

The Citizen then grabbed his cell phone and called 911.

He said, "Hello, police. An aggressive individual is invading my facility, and he has already injured several of my men. My place of business is 211 W. Convenient Drive, the huge complex on top of the hill. Hurry, I think I might be next."

The Citizen hung up and waited. The Thief ran towards the nearest elevator and went all the way up to the third floor. When the door opened, The Thief saw only a stupendously big room with The Citizen sitting behind his desk in a big chair looking away from The Thief. The Citizen swiveled his chair to reveal himself wearing a white dress shirt and red tie. In his right hand was a jar with a strange glowing wisp.

"Hand over the Aethereus Nucleo!" The Thief shouted.

"The Citizen said, "Normally, in any other circumstance, I would give this to you and let you go off on your merry ways. Unfortunately, while you have your job, I have mine."

The Thief said, "You do not get it. That thing can be the key to advancing humanity in energy-producing technology."

The Citizen said, "Really?"

"If you won't give it to me by choice." pulling his knife, The Thief proclaimed, "then I will take it by force, you *******."

While The Thief began his charge, The Citizen bent his right arm inward as The Thief was up in the air about to strike him. The Citizen clenched his hand into a fist (Durability: Space) and rammed his enclosed arm right into the knife. The small blade broke off upon impact. The Citizen's attack landed on The Thief's ribcage, and he extended his arm to propel the enemy away from him. The Thief doubled over and roared in pain. The Citizen walked up to The Thief with both arms behind his back.

The Thief said tensely, "I...I thin...ink you shaaattered some of my riiibbbs!"

The Citizen laughed and then exclaimed, "My Friend, you are up against one of the finest security systems in this entire country. I am impressed that you have survived a medical experiment that could shoot lasers from his face, vampire surgeons, living shadows, and even avoiding the giant, adapting robot. Do you think it was easy to get an adapting robot? It would have been difficult if this wasn't a storage facility filled with extraterrestrial and mystical objects. I have to protect everything, or these things could be used to destroy the world."

The Thief slowly closed his eyes as he slipped into unconsciousness. Two security guards came into the room, and they were mortified at very the sight. The very enemy that came in and beat them up was on the ground at the feet of their employer.

One of the men said, "Man, boss, you're one scary man when you want to be."

PASSAGE #6: A SPECIAL MORNING

The Citizen woke up and turned off an alarm that just went off. He lumbered out of his small bedroom to his even smaller bathroom across from it with nearly shut eyes. He grabbed his contact lens and put them in. After four minutes in the shower, The Citizen walked back to his bedroom. He put on a black t-shirt with a strange "R" made with a square, a circle, and a triangle. He also put on blue jeans and white socks.

He went to the kitchen to partake in a breakfast of two bagels, a banana, orange slices, and chocolate milk. He turned on the TV and saw a news reporter talking about the city after the battle between The Superhero and a giant monster a couple of days ago. The reporter thanked the city's champion for his effort. The Citizen changed the channel and watched cartoons until he finished eating his meal.

The Citizen turned off the TV and left his apartment room. He walked up to the roof to begin his favorite activity, a little morning ability training. He grabbed (Strength: Space) the air around the wooden crate full of bricks and threw it into the air. The wooden box flew about 20 feet in the air. As it started to descend, The Citizen pulled his right leg back (Strength: Nothingness) and, instead of his leg-breaking, he caught the crate with his leg without any damage. He kicked the box back into the air as it fell again. He stood still (Durability: Nothingness) and closed his eyes. The crate landed on his head, and like before, and it did not break. The Citizen took a deep breath and smiled, having gone through another successful exercise once again.

Before returning to his apartment, he noticed that dark clouds were out, and he just assumed that it was just going to rain. Suddenly, a brilliant light flashed across the sky and almost blinded The Citizen. Soon after, energy bolts rained from the sky, striking the many buildings in his neighborhood. The Citizen ran inside the apartment and up two floors to get back into his room. He thought that since the city was under attack, people would evacuate. His hometown had been attacked so many times that they had escape plans set in place for future crises. He grabbed a medical kit if he or others became injured while fleeing. He sensed that this attack was different, and he wanted to be ready for what could happen.

PASSAGE #7: THE SUPERHERO AND THE CITIZEN

People fled as their city fell into ruin because of a supernatural battle between good and evil. The Citizen found The Superhero in a crater after his fight with a mysterious adversary. His outfit was frayed, revealing parts of his bruised flesh. He was too injured to get out of the pool of dirt and cement that he created when he crashed. Luckily, The Citizen has a medical kit.

The Citizen said, "Don't move. I'm going to fix you up a bit."

In a faint tone, The Superhero replied, "Okay."

The Citizen pulled out his bandages and remedies from his coat pocket. The Superhero laid back quietly in his little marsh of urban debris as The Citizen tended to his wounds. The thoughts of healing this man were flowing through The Citizen's mind.

After a deep sigh, The Superhero spoke, "I tried my best to beat this villain, only to find out that I am an accomplice to my enemy's quest to destroy the city."

The Citizen just stared at him with his golden-brown eyes thinking of what to say, but he could not formulate a single sentence to comfort him.

The Superhero asked, "Please, tell me, what do you do when you are told that you would do something great, but you fail to achieve that greatness?"

The Citizen's mind was racing. Sweat appeared on his forehead and flowed right down to his round, brown cheeks. He could not think of anything. So, he told him the truth "I don't know."

Then The Superhero asked, "What do you do when your time to shine comes, but you can barely produce a spark?"

The Citizen said again, "I don't know."

The Superhero asked another question "Where is hope in the future when the hero cannot save this day?"

"I don't know.", The Citizen said, "No matter what I'm supposed to do, what my future holds, or what kind of opportunity appears. At the end of it all, I'm just a person trying every day to live my life and go against any challenge it brings to me."

The Superhero looked up towards the sky covered by clouds of smoke, and he thought about The Citizen's words. Soon, small rays of the sunlight filtered through the smoke, one of them landed on The Superhero. The Superhero felt something in him, something reborn. The Superhero rose above The Citizen and out of the pit.

"I understand now." The Superhero said, "Thank you for helping me in my time of need, but now I need to finish this."

The Citizen gave a thumbs up. The Superhero flew straight up towards his gray aura-coated foe that was in the air the whole time. Then the smoke-filled sky burst open with a vast blue flash as the battle ensued between the two warriors. The Citizen looked up with his eyes wide open, smiling at the action above. He left the ditch and kept running towards an evacuation point.

PASSAGE #8: THE RIDIFICCI LIFESTYLE

The Citizen and The Superhero sat on top of The Citizen's apartment to talk. After talking about some of their experiences during the villain's attack, The Superhero finally asked, "Do you have any powers?"

The Citizen replied openly, "Technically, I do. How could you tell?"

The Superhero said, "I remember you before from our official meeting when *we* stopped that thug together. You did something to take that man's weapon away from him."

The Citizen said smiling, "Well, that is what the *Ridificci Lifestyle* is all about."

The Superhero remarked, "Ridificci ...? What does ...."

The Citizen interrupted, "...that mean? I first take Latin word *ridiculum*, meaning absurd. Then mix it with *artifici*, meaning art. Now, it means "unique technique," at least to me, it does.

The Superhero asked, "What are these unique techniques?"

The Citizen explained, "My master only gave me

one lesson before leaving me to die in another dimension: *Make your own methodology*. So, while drifting in the metaphysical realm, I slowly learned the intricacy of how existence worked. With that knowledge, I developed the ability to turn my natural faculties into existential forces using concepts like time, probability, etc., as models for them."

The Superhero asked, "Can you give me an example of this ability?"

With a smile, The Citizen said, "Sure."

He walked toward his wooden crate, grabbed it (Strength: Space), and it flew into the air. As it started to descend, The Citizen pulled his right leg back (Strength: Nothingness) and caught it with his leg without any damage. The Superhero gasped at the sheer spectacle of it all.

The Citizen kicked it back in the air. As it fell again, The Citizen (Durability: Nothingness) stood still as The Superhero braced himself for the possibility of things going south. The crate landed on his head, and like before; it did not break. The Superhero clapped for the show, but The Citizen was not finished. He grabbed (Strength: Space) the air around the crate again and launched the box right back into the sky. This time, The Citizen pulled back his right arm (Strength: Causality) and punched the crate. The crate burst into pieces revealing the bricks inside. The Superhero could not believe his own eyes. How could a mere human break such material with his bare hands?

The Superhero shouted out, "That was amazing!"

As The Citizen was holding his blackened, bruised fist, The Citizen said, "I know, right, but... Owwww, that really hurts. I shouldn't have shown off."

The Superhero questioned, "Why aren't you a superhero?"

The Citizen replied, "It is simple. I do not want that kind of responsibility. I don't mind being a "Super- Samaritan" occasionally, but that kind of obligation can drive a man like me crazy."

In a downhearted tone, The Superhero said, "Oh, I see."

The Citizen said, "Being a superhero is not all that bad. I am just saying it is not meant for everyone. If one needs to help a fallen man out of a pit or to bandage him up, those are just as heroic as fighting a villain."

Before The Superhero could get a word in, a massive explosion sounded a few miles away, and The Superhero just flew off.

The Superhero said to The Citizen as he headed towards the explosion, "It was nice seeing you again, but you know a hero's work is never done."

The Citizen waved goodbye and walked back to his room.

PASSAGE #9: THE HEIRESS AND THE CITIZEN

The Citizen was running through a dungeon. He was trying to reach the end to get to the other side of a castle when he stumbled upon a brunette-haired woman in a tattered violet dress in a cell.

The woman said, whimpering, "Wh... who's there?"

The Citizen answered, "Just a citizen of totality, and you must be this heiress that the dictator kidnapped. The media had dubbed this incident the *Princess Crusade.* Every man, soldier, and mercenary outside are trying to rescue you."

The Heiress cried out, "Yes, please, let me out!"

The Citizen said, "No, it's a good idea to stay in here until someone comes for you, instead of roaming freely through this castle alone."

The Heiress said, "I won't be alone if I follow you."

The Citizen exclaimed, "That's a horrible idea. I am here because some man stole a certain item from my facility, and he was last seen in this castle."

The Heiress said with concern, "Really?"

The Citizen said, "Yeah. The dictator of this fortress hired him. I still cannot figure out this country's name. Anyway, I am getting off-topic. He is dangerous. If I must protect you, I cannot fight him *and* get what I am here for. So, I'll tell you what. When I'm finished, and you're still here, I'll bust you out and escort you to safety."

The Heiress explained, "I can protect myself if you can give me a weapon."

The Citizen moaned, "Fine."

The Citizen reached for the lock, grabbed it (Strength: Probability), and then flicked it. Soon, the object fell into pieces from rust, and The Citizen opened the cell. The Heiress, thrilled by her release, hugged The Citizen. The Citizen broke out of the hug and walked toward one of the dictator's unconscious soldiers. He took the soldier's rifle and walked back to The Heiress.

As he towered over her, The Citizen gave her the rifle and said, "Here. I hope that you get out of here safely."

The Heiress said, "Thank you and good luck finding your...missing item."

The Citizen pointed in the direction where she needed to go, and The Heiress showed that she understood with a nod. The Citizen ran in the opposite direction that The Heiress was going. When The Heiress turned toward the course of her escape, she saw that over twenty of the dictator's heavily armed soldiers were out cold. The Heiress stopped focusing on that and began to run for freedom.

PASSAGE #10: A TIME TO FIGHT

A new trespasser had infiltrated the facility. The Citizen had already called the police and waited. A woman with mint-dyed hair knocked down the door to his office, and her clothes were shredded by the fights she had to go through to get here. Standing in front of a large window, The Citizen turned around to face his newest interloper.

As he smiled, The Citizen said, "Hello, and what brings you to my office tonight, my weary friend? Could it be for The Path of Destiny?"

In shock, the woman replied, "How did you know that?"

Continuing to smile, The Citizen answered, "Well, that is a facility secret. What if you somehow escape from jail and come back here? You would have the element of surprise, and I would be at a disadvantage. Now, who are you, and why do you want to find the POD?"

The woman said, "That's not important, but I am chosen by fate to save the world. I need to find The Path of Destiny to gain access to...."

In a calm, monotone voice, The Citizen interrupted, "...The Monolith. A giant construct created by an ancient tribe to be the ultimate wish-granting tool. A device that can read your mind and even your soul to make your wish perfect."

In shock again, The Chosen One said, "You seem to know a lot about it."

In a lighter tone, The Citizen responded, "Well, I did spend ten years finding and protecting the POD and its portal. That is the only reason I became the manager of this place. It is why I enlisted monsters, failed experiments, and criminals into my workforce. It is why I must wear this awful tie."

The Chosen One said, "I am sorry if this responsibility is too much for you."

The Citizen responded, "Don't worry about it. One of my only solaces is that occasionally some audacious fool has the idea that they have the power or skill to get in here and get out.

In which case, 85% of those intruders die from being beaten, eaten, or cursed to death. Another 10% decide to retreat only to come back and get killed anyway. Then there are people like you, the 5% who proved to be a cut above the rest. Then I get up from my bed, get over here, and then release my frustration by ruining your hopes. Then I give you a consolation prize of 20 years of jail for breaking into a government-owned facility."

With confidence, The Chosen One roared, "If this

is what it comes down to. I guess I have no choice but to defeat you and make you reveal the thing I seek."

While the police arrived outside the facility, The Citizen interjected, "Whoa, Whoa, Whoa, calmed down. We don't have to fight, especially since the cops have already arrived."

As she began to glow with a bluish aura, The Chosen One said, "I am not letting my mission to save the world ends here. Let's do this!"

With sweat on his forehead, The Citizen exclaimed, "Are you serious? Listen, if you just give up, I promise that you'll get 15 years of prison, 10 with good behavior."

The Chosen One sprinted at him with incredible speed and pulled back her arms. The Citizen thought to himself that she would probably do some rapid jabs. The Citizen moved directly in front of his desk. The Chosen One released (Evasiveness: Time) a flurry of fists, but she could not believe that a big man like him could dodge with such incredible speed. As time seemed slow to him, The Citizen moved forward, passed all her punches, and punched her in the stomach. The Chosen One fell in pain.

The Citizen said, "So, can you now surrender?"

After coughing, The Chosen One yelled, "I must not give up!"

The Chosen One got back up and did a spinning kick (Durability: Space), only for her to bounce off him with all the power she exerted with that attack. It was not in vain, for the real power behind her kick was strong enough to knock The Citizen on his back, yelling in pain.

The Chosen One got up again and charged at the still screaming Citizen. She ran towards her enemy, readying another assault, and The Citizen used a low kick to knock her down once again. They both got back up, and The Chosen One charged at him. The Citizen bent his right arm inward and scanned for an opening. As she attacked with a right hook, The Citizen saw his chance. Her left side was vulnerable.

The Citizen then moved to the left and landed his attack on her exposed side. Then he extended (Strength: Existence) his right arm was enveloped by a bronzed, luminescent force and launched The Chosen One right into the wall. She became unconscious as she hit the ground. The security guards came in and grabbed her to take her to the police.

With annoyance in his voice, The Citizen said, "Why do you guys always come in after the fight?"

As the guards left with The Chosen One, one of them said, "Because we love to see you at work."

The Citizen asked them to wait a minute and went to his desk. He took a piece of paper to write down a message. He folded the paper and wrote, "Next time, make an appointment. We can talk."

He walked back to the guards and slipped the

message underneath a bracelet on her arm. He signaled them to take The Chosen One to the authorities.

As they left, The Citizen said to himself, "If she is the "Chosen One," then I'm afraid my life is now intertwined with her destiny."

End of Volume 1

VOLUME 2

Published October 24, 2018

PASSAGE #1: "WIND AFFINITY: SPACE" DAY

It's that time of the month again. The Citizen put his hand into a hat filled with paper strips. He pulled out a piece that said "space" and pulled another one that said "wind."

The Citizen said, "Hakehaha, I know what I am going to do today."

The Citizen ran to the roof, and he looked at the building on the other side of the street. He walked back from the edge to get a running start. He dashed to the corner, jumped (Wind Affinity: Space), and an invisible rift released a gust of wind underneath him. The blast thrust him to the roof of the other building.

Afterward, he proceeded to go around the city and use his new ability. He went downtown and decided to go to a diner with an outdoor counter for ice cream. He reached the restaurant, where he found a small group of teens littering their trash, cursing, and dancing around like monkeys. They were at the counter, but they were too distracted by their conversation to notice the cashier asking them what they wanted. After a minute, The Citizen got tired of waiting and sidestepped (WA: S). A gust of wind appeared from a rift behind the teens, and they struggled against it while The Citizen passed them. He asked for his favorite flavor, Peanut Butter Chip. After The Citizen bought it, he jumped (WA: S), and the wind blew him away. The teens screamed in shock, and The Citizen just chuckles on the roof, enjoying his ice cream.

The Citizen walked down an alley that is one of many hiding places for convicts, muggers, and even serial killers if you are unlucky enough. By the time he was halfway through the narrow pathway, a man had appeared from behind a group of trash cans. The Citizen yelped at the sight of his gun.

The man said, "Get ready. You're about to have the worst day of your life because it is going to be your last."

After a deep breath, The Citizen said, "Look, I do not want to sound like the one who likes to mock people, but... get ready for the worst day of *Your* life."

With a confused look, the man said, "That is the weirdest last words I ever... (WA: S)... heard?"

The wind blew the man upward, and as he fell, The Citizen readied himself to strike. Moments later, the police arrived to take the offender to the station. The man shook and kept crying about a vanishing man as he was carried off. The Citizen watched as he continued to walk back to his apartment.

PASSAGE #2: GOLDEN OPPORTUNITY

The Citizen ran toward one of the warehouses down at the pier as his pursuer chased him. He saw a sign that said "Caution: Explosives in Building." He removed it and went inside. In the warehouse, he hid behind a pile of crates. He was out of breath and waited until he heard metallic footsteps.

The Citizen ran behind one of the many piles of crates as he entered the building. His pursuer was an enormous man, made of gold. The Golden Man walked into the warehouse and looked around, shouting, "I know you are here."

The Citizen asked, "Why are you doing this? You were once an explorer. You're a man who believes that finding out the past will take our world into the future, and now you are turning people into gold."

The Golden Man said, "I am doing so much more than turning people into mere gold. I am evolving them into a new race, The Golden Organics."

The Golden Man continued to walk into the center of the warehouse, looking for him. The Citizen kept moving around the warehouse to avoid detection and maintain his dialogue.

The Golden Man said, "I wasn't exactly turned to gold at first but encased in it. I believed that I starved to death in a month, and soon, my golden coffin became my cocoon as I transformed years later into the shimmering being before you. The only thing that is still normal about me is this piece of lifeless flesh that I call a hand, still afflicted by the power that bauble gave me."

With a disgusted tone, The Citizen replied, "Yeah, that thing is pretty gross, man. You touch people with that, and it's all pale, thin, and it wobbles to and fro every time you move. Ack!"

The Golden Man said, "When I gained life again, I remembered hearing your conversation with your would-be "Master." I was enraged that you cleverly got your wish while we paid the price for ours."

The Citizen interjected, "So, let me guess, you want to make me suffer the same fate you experienced."

The Golden Man smashed through the empty crates that The Citizen was currently hiding behind. The Citizen was shocked as he walked forward. As The Golden Man walked towards The Citizen, he raised his horrific hand to deliver the final blow.

After a menacing laugh, The Golden Man uttered, "You were always too smart to be a pack mule."

The Citizen (Strength: Time) pushed The Golden Man, only to be immediately laughed at because his pursuer did not budge. The Golden Man tried to touch him with his hand once again, but The Citizen jumped back. The Golden Man continued to run his target, but he noticed that he was moving slowly away from The Citizen. This unseen force over each second continued to build up, pushing his golden body harder and harder away until eventually, he flew into crates filled with explosives. They all detonated, and The Citizen heard his pursuer's scream. The Golden Man got back up from the smoke and noticed huge cracks on his body.

After a snarl, The Golden Man said, "After you are turned into a Golden Organic, I am going remove your head, melt it down and use it to fill the cracks you made on my pure frame."

The Citizen remarked, "Well, next time, read the signs before you chase someone in a warehouse. Oh, wait. I took the sign down before I went in. Also, Golden Organic is a terrible name. Try to shorten it or make a portmanteau of two Latin words as I do."

With a savage roar, The Golden Man dashed towards The Citizen, but The Superhero crashed down from the ceiling. He slammed and crushed the Golden Man into pieces. The pieces were still moving around, indicating that he was still alive. The Citizen grabbed a plank of wood and scooped up the hand as the plank turned into gold. He dropped it into an empty crate, and it too was given a golden hide.

The Citizen sighed and said, "Thanks for taking

that guy down."

The Superhero said, "If it wasn't for that explosion, you could have been just like the others, turned into golden statues."

The Citizen remarked, "It is not too late. I learned from my old colleague that the victims are trapped in a golden shell. The transformation is super slow."

"Well then, let's get them out!" The Superhero said as he grabbed The Citizen and flew out of the warehouse. "By the way, your old colleague?"

The Citizen quickly responded with, "Long Story."

PASSAGE #3: ON-THE-SIDESHOW CAREER

The Citizen drew a crowd of people around him in front of the city's park fountain. He waved his arms and kept his turban from falling off his head. Next to the Citizen was a sign that said, "Supernatural Gimmicks and Wonders."

As he pulled out a knife, The Citizen said, "For my first act, I will throw this knife straight into the air and dodge it in the last second!"

The crowd moved back from him. The Citizen threw the knife and stood perfectly still as the small blade made its return trip. The group started to gasp at what was about to come. The Citizen took a deep breath. The knife soon was right on top of him (Evasiveness: Time), and it appeared to him that the blade slowed down mid-air long enough for him to step back just before the knife hit him. The crowd was cheering, applauding, and threw money into a confederate hat that was spray-painted brown.

The Citizen exclaimed, "For my next supernatural feat, I will float in the air!"

He jumped (Wind Affinity: Probability), and an unnaturally strong blast of air appeared. It blew him about 15 ft. into the sky for over a minute. The crowd once again cheered with amazement. The wind died down; The Citizen landed somewhat softly with both feet on the ground. He checked his hat to see it was overflowing with cash. He thought that it was time for the finale.

The Citizen said, "For my final act, I will disappear, and you will not be able to find me."

The Citizen jumped into the crowd (Evasiveness: Nothingness) and slowly became transparent. He lay low because he was still slightly visible, and nobody could see him. The public moved around amongst each other to find him. Soon, the people realized that he was gone. The audience slowly turned around to leave, only to see The Citizen was standing right behind them. The audience clapped at his unique trick and threw enough money into his hat that it overflowed.

As The Citizen walked away, he said to himself, "53...54...55... $73.76. It's just like what my master said to me once, "Concentration is the first and important step toward changing the universe."

PASSAGE #4: THE VAGABOND VS. THE CITIZEN

Wearing his Wapaloosie coat, The Citizen stands alone on an island with a grassy meadow with giant boulders placed around the place. Soon, The Citizen saw his opponent, an alleged swordsman known as The Vagabond. He was like a willow tree with eyes that made you feel like something was wrong in his life. His black outfit nearly matched his skin tone, and his hair reminded The Citizen of a freshly trimmed hedge back at his apartment. The Vagabond walked towards The Citizen slowly as he tapped on one of his two sheathed swords rapidly.

A helicopter flew above the two men. Its rotating blades generated a gust of wind that caused the grass to fly around the finalists. They were not bothered by it because they focused on each other with great intensity.

Through speakers on the helicopter, The Show Host yelled, "Vagabond! Plush!"

As soon as he heard his epithet, The Citizen sighed with shame.

The Show Host continued, "You are our show's finalists. You and 16 other competitors lived on your own harsh, personal section of our island for weeks until ten players gave up, and you two invaded the sections of 6 remaining opponents. You fought them in various challenges and took their banners to eliminate them from the game. This is your final challenge, a simple one-on-one battle to determine the winner! The battle is only over when someone is either knocked out or admits defeat! All methods are allowed except for murder. Oh! If you can, try to shout out your attacks! The audience loves that kind of stuff! So, are you two ready?!"

After both competitors acknowledged with a nod, the host shouted, "Then, Begin!"

The Citizen fell on his back and just laid there. The Vagabond ran toward The Citizen and pulled out a wooden sword.

The Vagabond shouted, "Straight Sla...!"

Somehow, The Citizen started moving toward his opponent on his back as if he had feet back there. Caught off guard, The Vagabond cringed as his adversary walked in on him at high speed. The Citizen moved his right leg up while beginning to spin on his back. As he got right in front of The Vagabond, The Citizen's leg made a full circle, and The Citizen kicked his opponent.

Humoring The Show Host's request, The Citizen shouted, "Hodag Horn!"

The Vagabond blocked the attack with his sword, but it shattered upon impact. The kick still got him in the guts. The Vagabond doubled over as The Citizen got up by sliding on his back upwards. The Vagabond stood slowly back up as well.

He asked The Citizen, "What in the world was that?"

The Citizen replied, "I used my coat to move."

The Vagabond said, "Your coat does what?"

The Citizen said, "Yeah, my coat can move around on its own."

The Vagabond argued, "Your coat doesn't make sense."

The Citizen interjected, "Some things do not need to make sense. They just have to work. Now, let's continue this match with another decent attack. Like this one...."

The Citizen ran into the ground, and Meredith moved him, making him slide on the nearly flat surface. The Vagabond pulled out his other sword, and The Citizen noticed lacerations on his body from nowhere. The Citizen stopped his attack and looked at The Vagabond to see a katana with a dark blue blade. He looked closely at the sword and saw the dust fragments were flying towards it. He felt the pieces in his flesh were digging back out to return to their source. It felt like glass being pulled out of him. Soon, all the shards reattached themselves to the blade itself as if they were pieces to a puzzle.

The Vagabond said boldly, "I see that you are taking an interest in my sword."

While grunting, The Citizen said, "Yeah, I noticed that your sword is just as interesting as Meredith."

"Yes, it is an awe-inspiring blade, not fit for direct conflict, but for long-range assault." The Vagabond explained, "This sword was once in a million pieces until scientists reconstructed it and they infused it with a unique magnetizing method. Though fragile, this sword will always be whole no matter the distance and will not combine with other metals or magnets. One swing can release a nearly invisible gust of shards onto my enemies, and those shards will return to become whole. This is my true sword, my true tool, my true soul, Firearm Dusk."

The Citizen said, "I talked about my coat, but I didn't ask you about your sword's backstory."

Before The Vagabond could provide a rebuttal, The Citizen fell on his belly and moved forward. The Vagabond started flailing his sword at the path in front of The Citizen, hoping to hit, but The Citizen was aware of his sword's function this time. He rolled side to side rapidly to maneuver most of the attacks. Soon, The Citizen was up close to The Vagabond, and he pulled back his right fist. He kicked the ground and uppercuts at The Vagabond, screaming, "Snoligoster Spear!"

For the second time, The Vagabond fell, and The

Citizen patted himself on the back. The Vagabond was frustrated. He tried to take another swing, but The Citizen slid up to The Vagabond and rolled on his back so that his coat could spin him. His legs slammed into The Vagabond with continuous rotation and senseless speed, yelling, "Walloping Whimpus!"

The Vagabond quickly recovered from the attack. He jumped in the air above The Citizen and swung rapidly to unleash his attack.

The Vagabond screamed, "Firearm Dusk's Hell Gale!!!"

There were too many shards to dodge. So, The Citizen swiftly removed Meredith, and it fled the scene. The Citizen took the attack head-on, and he felt his body being hit by a breeze of toothpicks.

The attack soon stopped, and The Citizen's clothes were covered in slash marks. Meredith returned to him like a loyal companion ready to aid its master or by coincidence. After looking at his minor wounds, The Citizen noticed small rips on his coat from The Vagabond's attacks. His right eye twitched, his teeth clenched, and his fists tightened. The Vagabond started to move back his arms with the sword to ready himself for a steady swing. Since his opponent was getting prepared, The Citizen took this opportunity to launch another attack. Like before, he fell on his back, and Meredith moved him toward The Vagabond. The Citizen started to move his legs by thrusting them rapidly at his foe.

The Citizen announced, "Here I come, Vaga-buddy! Whinnnntooossserrrrr!!!..."

The Vagabond said, "Firearm Dusk's...!"

The two competitors were near each other as both were about to finish calling the names of their attacks.

The Vagabond finished, "...Dragoon Beam!!!"

The Vagabond swung his sword, and the whole blade came off. The force of the swing distorted the katana into a serpentine form. The Citizen kept on kicking even faster and thrust his legs hastily. Before the attack hit, The Citizen traveled to the right by pushing his arm on the ground and dodged most of it. The attack grazed him, but he kept moving. He curved directly toward The Vagabond.

While The Vagabond was in shock, The Citizen gave out a final shout, "...Mauling!!!"

The Citizen kicked his enemy multiple times with considerable force in the stomach region. The Vagabond was utterly helpless against The Citizen's barrage. The Citizen gave him one final kick that launched the Vagabond into the air. When the Vagabond landed, he was on his back, unconscious. The Citizen stood up and walked toward his opponent, and The Firearm Dusk quickly regained its blade.

The Citizen said, "Sorry, man. I never wanted to be the winner. I just wanted the little figurine that is attached to the trophy."

With a raspy voice, The Vagabond said, "Then don't worry...."

Then as he continued, The Vagabond's blade fell off to reveal a hidden taser, and he jammed it into The Citizen's leg and zapped him.

The Vagabond finished, "... I just want the prize money."

The Citizen collapsed and was unable to move. The helicopter above the match descended upon the battlefield and landed a few yards away from the fighters. The Show Host and some cameramen ran to see the winner.

To the many cameras around him, The Show Host announced, "Congratulations, Vagabond! You are this season's champion of *Isolation to Invasion*!"

The Vagabond received his trophy and prize money. With respect for The Citizen, he pulled off the artifact from the top of the prize and tossed it right beside The Citizen.

With the last bit of consciousness, The Citizen thought, "I shouldn't have taken my brother's bet to use only Meredith in this fight. But...At least... I ...I... Have the...the...Artifaaa..."

The Citizen (Destructiveness: Existence) reached out for the statuette, and a reddish-brown, ethereal mass appeared. It engulfed and disintegrated the figurine, and no one noticed because all eyes were still fixated on The Vagabond. So, with that, The Citizen finally passed out.

PASSAGE #5: A TIME TO TALK

As The Citizen opened the door, The Chosen One barged into his apartment. The Citizen tried to run toward the window, but The Chosen One moved in front of him to kick him right into his armchair, where it broke.

The Chosen One said, "We need to talk."

After taking a deep breath, The Citizen said, "You came to the right place, *Incomiber*."

The Chosen One sat on the couch while The Citizen was getting refreshments from his kitchen. She noticed a disassembled sniper rifle in a glass frame on a wall. Next to it was a photo with a group of boys in military school uniforms. She walked up to it to see if The Citizen was in it. The Chosen One saw a boy with similar features to The Citizen with another slightly older boy who looked almost like him.

She turned a tad to the right and gasped at the fact that she never noticed a suit of armor with stone plating on the shoulders, shins, and breastplate in a massive glass case at the corner of the room. The helmet appeared to have small horns like a deer made of stone. She walked up to it and read the plaque between its feet. It said, "The Armor of The Heuristic Knight-

Obtusehart." On the palm of the right gauntlet was a picture of knights. Like the other picture, a youth with Citizen-Esque features was present wearing the same armor she saw on display. He was standing next to the same young man from the other picture. The Chosen One was now even more confused about who she was dealing with.

The Citizen reached out (Reachability: Dimension) his arm into a portal to give a cup of fruit punch to The Chosen One through another portal next to her. The Citizen walked to the living room with his beverage and a plate of saltine crackers and pepperoni. He sat on the couch while The Chosen One sat on the other end, and they both took a sip before having their conversation.

The Chosen One asked, "I want to know...What the hell is that?!"

As he looked up to see his coat moving around the ceiling, The Citizen answered, "That's just Meredith. Don't mind her, as you were saying."

Regaining her composure, The Chosen One said, "Ahh... right. Anyway, I wanted to ask what you know about The Monument."

The Citizen complied and said, "It all started about 11 years ago. I was in the transcended planes after 300 years, or was it 30? Anyway, many years of training... You see, time doesn't necessarily exist there. So, I had plenty of time to gain my...."

The Chosen One interrupted, "...Ridificci Lifestyle."

The Citizen asked, "How did you know that?"

The Chosen One answered, "You're, and my friend the superhero of this city told me."

With a depressed sigh, The Citizen explained that he learned about a great civilization after his training and reconciliation with his master. Like many other advanced, ancient societies, they died out and left behind their most remarkable inventions. These tools could change anything in the physical world. They used them to terraform the land, revert disasters, and even make miracles. They needed an "operating system" to control these objects' power and understand their request. So, they made artificial "spirits" to inhabit these devices like The Citizen's own master.

After the ancient people's fall, the operating systems gained true sentience and transcended their abilities beyond our physical realm. Luckily, most people in the present put the ideas of wish-granting items into the domain of folklore and fairytales. So, most people do not bother. As gratitude for his master's training, The Citizen made it a goal to hunt down and eliminate the items that kept these spirits sealed. They wished to be freed from their mundane bind to live beyond our reality completely. He already destroyed 13, and only a few remained, including The Monument.

The Citizen said, "I'm sorry for talking so much,

but you did ask about what I know."

After drinking more juice, The Chosen One said, "I do not mind."

The Citizen replied, "But now the question that I have to ask is, what is your goal? You asked me about what I know. It should be fair that you tell me the same."

As she stood up, The Chosen One said, "I... I need to figure out what my destiny is. A few weeks or so ago, I was a regular person with a regular job, living in an apartment like yours, and lived an everyday life until I found myself talking to some older man. He told me that I must use the power of fortune and seek The Path of Destiny to know my fate. Then he died at my feet from a dozen arrows in his back."

The Citizen uttered, "Hmmmm, that is quite a predicament. You had a choice of either keeping your old life or to forsake all to find out something that could be grander."

The Chosen One replied, "Yes, but my choice isn't terrible. By putting my complete trust in destiny, I can unleash a power that allows me to achieve great feats."

The Citizen said, "It seems that you did not regret your choice, but let's get to the bone of the matter. You want The Monument, but I am in your way because of my desire to destroy it to free the spirit within the device. Fortunately for you, I cannot access it because I am not chosen for a higher purpose, and the POD only lets one of those through its threshold."

The Chosen One interjected, "Why don't we just go there now. I can get my answer, and then you can destroy it."

The Citizen replied, "Hold on, I am still dealing with the damage you have done to my employees and workplace. If you think that I am going to let you back in without any form of compensation, then you must be thinking that we are friends or something."

The Chosen One cried out, "Please, we have to have a compromise! I need it to know what the future holds for me."

With a smirk, The Citizen pulled out a map. He stated, "I know how we can compromise. Listen, if you can bring me the item on this map and come to my office, we can both get what we want."

PASSAGE #6: JUST A NIGHTMARE

A gray sun rose on a monochromatic world. A young boy and girl ran to a shed on top of a hill. The children went in it and shut the door behind them. The boy huffed and puffed as the girl's tears dripped from her rosy cheeks and black locks. The boy regained the air in his lungs and started to move the tools and equipment to block the door. The girl kept crying, but she soon stopped as the boy hugged her tightly. The girl coughed profusely, and then the boy cried out inaudible words to the girl as tears fell from his own eyes.

The pair then heard hard knocks from the door. They were loud like thunder, and the voices sounded like the growls of beasts. The girl coughed even louder as blood slowly seeped out of her mouth. The boy moved in front of the girl to protect her. The blockade fell onto the floor as the door burst into dust and tall fiendish figures appeared. Their bodies were covered in darkness except for their pale, gray heads with hair crawling like bugs. Their void-like eyes stared not at the boy but the girl.

The boy ran at them. One of the monsters dashed at him, and it grabbed him as the others held the girl. The pair struggled free and scampered out the door. As they reached the foot of the hill, the two kids were both caught in an explosion. The boy took most of the blast to protect the girl. The couple collapsed from the pain, and the girl coughed some blood. The boy's legs and lower back were covered in flames. The creatures moved towards the children inconsistently as some ran straight, others moved side to side, and some just teleported anywhere they wished. The boy could not do anything except close his eyes as the monsters stood right on top of them. The boy shut his eyes tighter and tighter until the boy turned into The Citizen.

The Citizen woke up, took a deep breath, and went to his bathroom. After turning on the lights, he looked at the mirror and realized that his contact lenses were still on. He took off his them. His golden-brown irises turned black. The pupils turned luminous orange and into the shape of an "R" made up of a square, circle, and triangle appeared within them. After that moment of sight, his view became distorted and covered with various otherworldly images before it all became blank. The Citizen muttered, "I still can't believe that these are what my eyes look like now. No matter how smart one's wish is, there is always a consequence."

He turned off the bathroom lights and walked out. Using his memories, He returned to his bedroom but dropped to the floor next to the bed. He yawned and went back to sleep.

PASSAGE #7: THE TOUR

The Citizen walked down a hallway with another man. He was leading him to more essential parts of his storage facility. Of course, he was slightly relieved because his big sister was supposed to be on this tour too, but she had other businesses to attend to. They went to the elevator, and The Citizen pressed the B1 button.

The tour began with the mineral section. The Citizen showed the man all the peculiar rocks and stones that the government had found over the years. There were meteorites, rare jewels, and even some of those minerals he got before he fled from the earth elemental. The man took a closer look at some yellow rocks, but The Citizen advised him not to go near them because they were toxic. So, the man backed off and went with The Citizen to the next section.

The Citizen showed off some serums, compounds, and potions made by mad scientists and deemed too dangerous for mass production in the chemical section. The Citizen played a little joke with the man by tossing a vial at him. The man dropped it, and it broke as it hit the ground, releasing a gas. The man tried to cover his mouth in a panic, but The Citizen said to relax and breathe it in. The man did what he said, and he noticed that the odor smelled like peaches. The Citizen chuckled as they moved on.

The two men had arrived at the operation room. The Citizen explained that this was where they do autopsies on things that were neither human nor any other creature known to humankind. There, they performed experimental surgeries. This was also the domain of some of The Citizen's more residential employees, the vampire surgeons. The vampires were in the middle of operating on a dead, unknown creature while drinking its blood. The man felt squeamish from looking at this display. So, The Citizen decided to move on with the tour.

After several more sections, they reached one of The Citizen's favorite parts, the mystical artifacts section. This was his favorite because he helped collect this fantastic assortment of mystic tools, from sorcerer staves to fairy charms. The Citizen showed the man his most significant find, a stone arch with five gems around it, The Path of Destiny. He enlightened the man that this magical gateway only opens to ones who have a significant connection to destiny. He tried to get in, but he could never succeed. Trying to keep up with the schedule, The Citizen moved on to the last section of the facility, The Zoo.

This section was on the last floor, and as they left the elevator door, the man's mouth dropped. This section was filled with creatures of all sorts, most from mythologies from Chupacabra to Manticores. The Citizen explained that sometimes in either his or other government exploits, encounters of the supernatural variety are imminent, usually ending with their homes or lives destroyed. The government put them here until they could be sent to their new habitat. The creatures looked and roared at The Citizen in admiration or fear as the two left and went back to the elevator.

The two men arrived back at the main office. That was when the man asked to make a private call. The Citizen left the room saying to press the green button to close the window shades and lock the door. As The Citizen left the room, the man pushed the button, and it did all that The Citizen said it would. The man pulled out his cell phone. He looked through his contact list until he found and hit the "Wife" button. He pressed it, and the phone rang.

As the person answered with a hello, the man said (Hearing: Space), "Hello, Mrs. President."

The President said, "Oh, Good afternoon, Mr. Vice President. How is the tour with my little brother doing?"

The Vice President replied, "The tour was certainly intriguing. I don't know why I must visit my brother-in-law alone. He always seemed off to me."

The President asked, "What happened to the security squad I sent with you?"

The Vice President said, "The last time they came to this place, one of them was eaten by an alien!... Or was it a manticore... Or maybe it was a squid man? Anyway, they said I'd be safe as long I stayed next to the manager. He's like a monster king or something."

The President said, "Oh relax, dear. You're acting like he is planning to kill you. Even though he could with no effort and not leave any evidence behind pointing to him."

After whimpering, The Vice President said, "Ok, now I want to get out of this place. I read the file on this place, and I believed only half of it. After the tour, I'll never doubt files under "Level 5 Classified" ever again. There are monsters and former criminals here, and I don't know why our daughter loves him so much."

The President stated, "He is family, and he is not the kind to use his power truly malevolent reasons. He could've been a criminal, and no one could stop him. He even knows it, but he chose a life of peaceful existence."

After a long sigh, The Vice President said, "Your right, and that is why you're running this country. Anyway, I should go out there and stop thinking that he could melt me with his heat vision...wait... he doesn't have heat vision, right. Never mind, see you tonight, honey."

The President exclaimed, "Goodbye."

The Vice President put his cell away and readied himself to see his brother-in-law. The Citizen was standing in the hallway listening to the whole conversation through a rift in space. He smiled, knowing that he was trying to see him in a different light. The Citizen headed toward his office door to see The Vice President with a smile.

PASSAGE #8: WAPALOOSIE WALKING

The Citizen reached the city's tallest building with his coat, Meredith, and placed the furry sleeve on the wall. It reacted and started to climb up the structure. Meredith pulled The Citizen onto the building wall and started to carry him up. The bystanders gasped as Meredith kept on moving. The Citizen stood still as he observed the city while the bystanders gawked at him.

4th Floor-The bystanders talked to The Citizen, asking him if he was alright. The Citizen only replied that he was enjoying the view. The bystanders did not understand his response. They just assumed that he was delirious, and someone called the police and fire department.

7th Floor- The police arrived only to leave immediately because they knew The Citizen too well. The same thing happened when the firefighters arrived. They all knew that whatever The Citizen was doing, he could handle it.

13th Floor- The Citizen looked in the inner pockets of Meredith and took out a bag of trail mix. He snacked on the assortment of nuts and candy as he looked at the traffic. Cars beeped, trucks honked, and sirens were heard all around him. He was glad he doesn't drive that often.

27th Floor- A man just snatched another man's wallet right out of his hand. The Citizen saw and thought he could lend a hand in this situation. He pulled out a coin from his pants pocket and (Accuracy: Probability) threw it. It hit a bird, and the small animal spiraled down onto the street. The bird flew right in front of a cyclist, and the poor cyclist turned right into the man with the stolen wallet. The Citizen chuckled until that bird he hit came at him, pecking and squawking. He swatted at it until it eventually left.

64th Floor- The sun was setting and bathing the city with the glow of twilight. The Citizen grabbed a camera from out of his coat and took a picture of the astonishing sight. Soon, his cell phone started to ring, and he answered it. His friend, The Geologist, asked him to remember The Earth Elemental from a few months back. Suddenly, The Citizen's eyes widened as he heard a huge rumbling sound.

78th Floor- The Earth Elemental had reached the city and was currently wrecking the place with its new and impressive size. It grew to the size of two humpback whales and was searching for its children. Those minerals that The Geologist and Citizen took were somehow The Earth Elemental's eggs. The Citizen suggested that the eggs should be returned. Unfortunately, they were already converted to powder for a new-age medical treatment. The Citizen frowned.

87th Floor- The Citizen was upside down for four floors, and he lost his trail mix. The Superhero had arrived on the scene a few minutes ago and fired energy beams at The Earth Elemental. They duked it out right in front of The Citizen's eyes, and he grabbed his camera again to take some pictures. Boulders and energy beams were flying everywhere. The mountainous beast roared with thunderous anger, and The Superhero glowed up to prepare a powerful attack. The Earth Elemental doused him with a torrent of stone and rock, but the blue light cut through the assault. Enveloped by the attack, the Earth Elemental roared one last time before it shattered into fragments.

Roof- The Superhero just finished talking to The Citizen about how excellent his finishing move against The Earth Elemental was. The Superhero offered to fly him down, but The Citizen declined. The Superhero flew down to help move the rocky remnants of the creature. The Citizen called back The Geologist and told him that the crisis had been averted for now. He went back down all way down to the...

...Ground Floor.

PASSAGE #9: TALES OF THE IVORY ROAMER- PART 1

The Citizen knocked on a door covered with stickers of unicorns, rainbows, and smiley faces. He heard a little girl's voice replying to come in, and he opened the door with a smile to see a little girl with brown pigtails in bed, shouting, "Uncle!"

The Citizen said, "Hey! How is my girl! I know that you were expecting mom or dad to tuck you in, but our President and Vice had an emergency conference. So, they asked me to come down here to put you to bed, but without reading you one of my stories."

The Pigtailed Girl giggled and cheered as The Citizen sat down on the end of her bed. He read from a sheet of paper:

"Tales of The Ivory Roamer"

Part 1: The Return Trip Begins

The story starts with a white-armored guardian protecting a gateway between the physical world of light and the metaphysical realm of darkness. He was given magical powers and a white shield that was as bright as the stars. He was the perfect guard physically, but his mind was undisciplined. He was but a mere child in his soul. He was given this task because he was an orphan. The original guardians who watched over the gate wanted a warrior to look after the gate. So, they enchanted the boy with magic that made him powerful enough to defend the great doorway. The former guardians left the boy with a shield and explored the world.

He fought many enemies who sought the mysteries behind the gate, but all had failed. The White Guardian grew restless over the years. He never asked to carry such a burden. One day, he heard a soothing voice and looked towards the origin of the sound. It was a lady covered in robes like the former guardians of the gateway. She told him not to fear her, for she is a child of one of the guardians, and she came to take his place. The White Guardian happily relinquished his position to her. The man walked away, and the lady laughed maniacally as she broke the many chains on the gate. The White Guardian ran back to stop her but was too late. She released the darkness of the metaphysical realm. The lady said she was not going to be the guardian of the gateway but the herald of the darkness within it. Her outfit became pitch black. She said that she was now The Ebon Priestess. With the power of the shadows, she striped The White Guardian of his armor and shield and sent him flying. The White Guardian landed far away from the gate, and he saw all the damage that it was causing.

So, he decided to travel back to the gate. Just then, a monster of shadows appeared to kill him for The Ebon Priestess. He grabbed a large log and charged at the beast. He imbued the trunk with his power with the magic within and slammed it into his attacker. The monster roared in pain and swiped him away to a tree. The beast pounced at him while The White Guardian lifted the log and jammed it into the monster's mouth. It died and vanished.

The White Guardian found the white cape he wore lying next to him; he picked it up, turning it into a makeshift coat. The White Guardian had now become The Ivory Roamer. The two things that he had learned from this event were this. An undisciplined mind has no place while you have responsibilities and when tragedy strikes, always move forward through it.

The End

Before The Citizen could start part 2, his niece was already asleep. He got off the bed, turned off the light, and quietly left the room as he heard her snoring. He looked back at the door and smiled, thinking that he would continue to tell her the rest of the story next time.

PASSAGE #10: IMPORTANT MESSAGES

The Citizen checked his mail and found a letter with a wax seal. The wax seal had a crest in the form of a helmet in the shape of the horse's head. He opened the letter, and it said:

To the person addressed, you are cordially invited to a wedding between Princess...

The Citizen crumbled it, knowing precisely what it was going to say. Then he checked his computer and found an email from a friend. He saw the email tagline being "Princess Crusade 2". He clicked it and read the message:

Hello Old Friend,

It has been a while. I need your help. An event is about to happen that will affect our country and others. You heard of the dictator who kidnapped the heiress of that big corporation several months ago. My inside source told me he plans to kidnap the president and other world leaders. He said that "The Princess Crusade" was a mere test run, and he will not lose so quickly next time. He did not prepare for every contingency. When I contacted the former hostage, she mentioned a man with the same physical features as you. Now, I am asking you to assist me with your talent. If we strike now, we can prevent another event like this before it happens again. We both serve to keep our country safe. So please, lend me your aid. Contact me through the number attached to this message. We'll meet up and leave immediately.

Your friend, ...

The Citizen was interrupted by a ringing from his phone. He picked it up and answered it. That was when he heard heavy breathing on the other end.

The Citizen said reluctantly, "Ahhhh, Hello?"

The Chosen One exclaimed, "Listen up...huff...I got it. I got the item!

The Citizen said, "Oh... That's great!"

The Chosen One stated, "I will be back to you in five to ten days."

The Citizen expressed, "I know that you have been waiting for this chance to know your fate, but I might not be around for a while."

The Chosen One said furiously, "What?! You said that we get what we both want if I bring this item to you. And now you are not going to be at the facility. Why?"

The Citizen declared, "I have to help a friend, and this could affect a lot of lives. I hope that you can understand this."

After a deep breath, The Chosen One said, "Ok, but when can you meet up again?"

The Citizen replied, "I am not sure myself, but. If I do not call you back within 30 days, go to my facility with the password that I am about to tell you. But don't go until after 30 days of my absence, or my staff will kill you."

With a grunt, The Chosen One said, "Very well, goodbye."

He took the card with the phone number from his pen pal's letter. He dialed the number and waited for his pen pal to answer. He heard a "Hello" and said, "Hey, when can we get started?"

End of Volume 2

VOLUME 3

Published February 19, 2019

PASSAGE #1: INFILTRATION

Wearing black Op attire, The Citizen and his friend, a spy who contacted him, ran towards a fortress. Beyond the forcefield, they saw a big hanger with vehicles. The Citizen laid his hand on the forcefield to feel the warmth and flow of energy creating the barrier.

The Spy asked, "Okay, how did you get through the barrier the first time. It took several days to break through this, and I am guessing that it has been updated."

The Citizen replied, "That is an easy one. I did this."

The Citizen pressed firmly on the barrier (Evasiveness: Probability), and the forcefield started to become distorted and staticky. The Citizen grabbed The Spy as they both slipped through before it worked correctly again. The Spy was relieved that they made it through, and he ran ahead, and The Citizen swiftly followed him. Before they could reach the hallway, a small squad of ten soldiers emerged from that hallway. They encircled them and pointed their guns, and then a woman wearing a black balaclava moved in front of the soldiers.

The balaclava woman exclaimed, "All right, what are

you two doing... here? Wait, I remember you."

The Citizen said, "Really?"

With concern, The Spy asked, "Do you know this woman?

The Citizen responded by shrugging his shoulders upward as the balaclava woman revealed herself as The Heiress. The Citizen and Spy were shocked and asked why she was here with these guys. She had been sending these mercenaries into the dictator's fortress for months since her liberation. When she was told that the dictator planned to kidnap others, she could not stand the idea of another person suffering from the same experience that she went through. So, she got her men to smuggle her in and planned to apprehend him. She did not expect the man who released her last time to come here this time. The Citizen explained that he was here to support his friend to do the same thing, and The Spy suggested that they work together. While blushing, The Heiress agreed with him.

An anonymous voice said, "If you want to achieve in this endeavor, you'll need my help."

Then a woman with unruly, raven hair emerged from a pile of crates. The mercenary squad aimed all their guns at her. The Spy calmly walked towards the stranger and told everyone that she was his inside source, a scholar of sorts.

The dictator forcefully employed The Scholar.

She was the one who created the forcefield and improved the dictator's already impressive stock of weapons and technologies. She managed to contact The Spy a while back and made a deal of giving her freedom in exchange for information. With some introductions out of the way, The Scholar suggested crippling the dictator by destroying his forcefield generator. Without her to maintain it, the dictator would lose his first line of defense. The second thing that is crucial to the dictator is his weapon storage. The last is his computer terminal filled with sensitive files and data.

The Spy suggested that this group split up into three teams to destroy their three targets. The Spy and three mercs would find, copy, and erase all the files from the terminal. The five of the other mercs should destroy all weapons in storage. The last two mercs and The Citizen would accompany The Heiress and The Scholar and destroy the forcefield generator. Everyone agreed, even The Heiress, who wanted to go with The Spy. The Scholar told The Spy where the terminal was, and the mercs knew the weapon storage was close by. The Scholar and her team started to leave for the forcefield generator.

With a smile, The Citizen said, "Don't get caught."

As he smiled back, The Spy said, "Protect them and stay safe."

PASSAGE #2: DESTINY'S DARK CHAMPION

As The Citizen, Scholar, and Heiress were about to destroy the forcefield generator, The two mercenaries guarding the entrance fell to the ground before an imposing figure. The trio turned to see a man with dark, orange hair and beard in regal attire.

After gasping, The Scholar exclaimed, "It's the dictator!"

As he started to glow a darkish red color, the dictator said, "Oh my dear, I am far beyond a mere wise, charismatic, warmongering leader. I was born under a hungry star. I have a destiny that will engulf all others. I am a chosen one who ascended from the darkness, The Dark One."

The Citizen said, "Huh, another one."

After shifting his focus to The Citizen, The Dark One said, "you met the other chosen one. The one also destined for a higher purpose."

The Citizen said, "Yeah, we talked, we fought, we talked again, we made a deal, and we talked again only by phone."

The Dark One asked, "You fought him?"

The Citizen replied, "Yeah, I fought "Her." Although our "fight" was a bit underwhelming. I immobilized her in about a minute."

The Dark One clenched his teeth and ran at The Citizen with a fierce red aura. The Citizen (Durability: Nothingness) raised his arms to block as The Dark One rammed into him. The Dark One's volley of punches hit The Citizen, but each impact seemed to be neutralized by an unseen force. He jumped away from The Citizen and charged back at him with more power. They (D: N) went through the room wall, but The Dark One started punching him through another wall. The Citizen was beginning to feel The Dark One's vigorous assault as they broke through one more barrier and reached the garden in the center of the fortress. The Citizen fell over in a flower bed, moderately injured by The Dark One's attack.

With his aura still blazing, The Dark One said, "Tell me that what you said about your fight the other chosen one was blasphemous. Tell me that you did not beat her or that she was some charlatan."

In a panic, The Citizen uttered, "Look, she seemed to be the real deal. She gave a similar speech you gave us. She glowed blue and ran to attempt to punch me rapidly like what you just did now. I was doing my job at the time. So, I subdued her before she caused more damage to my place of business."

The Dark One attacked him (D: N) again with a kick in the stomach, and The Citizen stood firm unaffected. The Dark One readied himself for another attack, but The Citizen enclosed his right arm inward and rammed into him with it. The Citizen extended (Speed: Causality) his arm to launch The Dark One away with incredible swiftness. The Dark One slowly stood up, grunting the whole time.

The Dark One said, "My destiny should have protected me from such absurd attack. MY DESTINY should have decimated you the moment I landed my first blow."

The Citizen explained, "I guess that my lifestyle's power is messing up your destiny somehow."

The Dark One asked, "What lifestyle is that?"

The Citizen answered, "I get this question a lot. I don't want to sound prideful, but I answer because my lifestyle is pretty cool. My Ridificci Lifestyle allows me to turn my qualities into concepts that control our universe."

With a new red blaze enveloping him, The Dark One shouted as he charged, "DO NOT GIVE ME SUCH AN ABSURD ANSWER!!!!"

The Citizen pulled back (Water Affinity: Causality) his fist. The Dark One just laughed at The Citizen at his display of defiance. Before The Dark One realized what he was going to do, The Citizen thrust his fist, and a powerful jet of water came forth. The Dark One was engulfed in his attack. His red aura faded, but it still protected him from most of the assault as he flew right through several trees. The Citizen attempted to apprehend The Dark One. The Citizen heard "Lookout" and jumped out of the way of bullets from some of the mercenaries. He was surprised to see the mercs holding The Heiress and Scholar hostage. Then more of The Dark One's men showed up with rifles aimed at the trio.

In his last moments of consciousness, The Dark One exclaimed, "Do you understand what I meant by my destiny will engulf all others. It's because anyone who submits to me or I have beaten, I can absorb their destiny, and they become subjugated to my will. I also get stronger and luckier, but I am not at the level I need to beat your... Lifestyle. Minions! Let them all go. I need to recover. Farewell."

The newly subjugated mercs kept their guns on the hostages as The Dark One fled. Soon his minions followed, The Citizen tended to the ladies, and they were both okay. So, they decided to destroy the forcefield generator even though The Dark One would probably flee to a new location.

PASSAGE #3: THE PROPOSITION

The banquet hall was filled with the sound of applause. While The President, wearing a white suit, spoke about the endeavors from recent events, The Citizen, Scholar, and Heiress sat at the same table. They were waiting to receive awards for their services to the country and the world by preventing a big crisis.

After a small squee, The Heiress said, "I can't believe this is happening, not even my folks have awards from the president, and they own a global company."

The Citizen said, "Yeah, all I ever got from my sister was protection from being tested and prodded, and a tiny slither of nepotism."

The Heiress asked, "Anyway, what are you two going to do now? I won't be running the family company until my parents believe I am ready. They say I am not ready for business and spend too much time and money on myself, but I have taken online business classes. I believe I'm ready."

After sighing, The Citizen answered, "I must go back to my job as manager of a storage facility."

The Scholar said, "I do not have a job, but I do

have a proposal that you two might be interested in."

As both The Citizen and she looked at each other and back at The Scholar, Heiress said, "We're listening."

The Scholar continued, "I want to take the dictator, but it would require your resourcefulness and your unique abilities."

Once again, both The Citizen and Heiress stared at each other and looked at The Scholar firmly. Then both agreed with her idea. The Heiress wanted to stop that madman since she got away the first time. The Citizen believed he would eventually be tasked to help take him down. While talking, they did not realize that The President spoke their names to come up the stage. The spotlights turned to them, and they immediately walked up. Each of them received a medal and a certificate. The audience clapped. The three with The Spy from another table took pictures with The President and returned to their seats.

PASSAGE #4: THE CHOSEN ONE VS. THE CITIZEN - REMATCH

The Chosen One unleashed (Evasiveness: Space) many punches at The Citizen, but her attacks phased right through him. She used a low kick to trip The Citizen, but it still did not work. The Chosen One jumped away from him and kept her distance. The Citizen was glad that they were fighting in a pocket dimension because he could not afford more damage to his facility because of her.

The Citizen exclaimed, "Look, I know you "Chosen" types are sensitive, but I am in no mood for an impromptu fight."

The Chosen One shouted, "Then you wouldn't mind letting me defeat you."

The Citizen said, "Uhhh no. I learned from the Dark One that you people can affect after your encounters. In his case, he could absorb other people's destinies and enslave them. Sorry, but you have to beat me fair and square."

The Chosen One stampeded towards him. The Citizen raised his hand in the air and swung (Electricity Affinity: Dimension) it down as he yelled,

"Enough!" The Chosen One was engulfed by a portal created by The Citizen and got spat out in electrical energy. A blue light warded it off before it caused real damage, but The Chosen One still felt some pain.

The Chosen One asked, "If you were able to do stuff that, why didn't you end him?"

The Citizen explained, "There was a hostage situation, and I couldn't do anything. It was as if fate was on his side or something."

The Chosen One dashed to punch him. The Citizen (Durability: Nothingness) stood still with his arm raised to block her fist. She pulled back her fist, and a blue mass emerged from it. It changed into an enormous fist, and she slammed it right into him. The Citizen was sent flying, wailing in pain. He landed on the ground and continued to cry out as The Chosen One slowly walked towards him.

The Chosen One exclaimed, "While I was at that temple you sent me to, I faced a guardian that pushed me to my limits. I imagine you sent me to my doom, and this power came from that feeling. The power to manifest tools that are destined for any situation. With this, I will prove that I am strong and save this world."

The Citizen rose as The Chosen One used her new power and manifest rigid-looking ax. She swung (Strength: Existence) it, and a strong force burst out of him, breaking the weapon. The Citizen pressed (Destructiveness: Causality) a finger on her stomach.

Then a tiny shockwave pushed The Chosen One away, and she breathed heavily.

The Citizen said, "Now that you hopefully got that violent tendency out of your system, can we get back to the reason why we went through the POD in the first place."

The Citizen looked at the dark, purple monument in front of them. Angrily, The Chosen One stood up and turned to it. She then wished to know her destiny. The Monolith glowed and spoke. Her fate was to bring a new era to this world but only after defeating The Dark One. The world was going to change, and either she or The Dark One would steer its course. First, she needs to amass more power and build a team to aid her journey. It said that this was her destiny and the light from it faded.

As he took out a piece of paper, The Citizen said, "Well, that's slightly redundant. Anyway, Hey, I got a wish, and it is to have a portable portal to this location."

The Monolith said, "Oh, it is you. You have finally come to free me."

Pulling out fragments of an artifact from his pocket, The Citizen said, "Yeah, would have been here sooner, but I have to free one of your brethren."

The Monolith uttered, "Is that from...."

The Citizen replied, "Yeah, it is."

The Monolith asked, "How? I was told it would be nearly impossible to get it."

As he pointed to The Chosen One, The Citizen answered, "She did it. She isn't The Chosen One for nothing."

As it laughed, The Monolith said, "Your master has taught you well."

Pressing his hands on The Monolith, The Citizen said, "Hahakeha, Yeah. Anyway, the portal."

The Monolith replied, "It is at your office for one-time use."

"Excellent," The Citizen said. He touched (True Destructiveness: Existence) The Monolith as he turned to The Chosen One, "Hey, could you carry me out after this transaction?"

The Chosen One felt a strong pulse emanating from him. An enormous reddish-brown substance emerged from The Citizen and violently wrapped around The Monolith. The Monolith began to crack, and light emerged from the cracks. The Monolith said, "Thank You," as it disintegrated into rubble. The Citizen sat down in a weakened state. The Chosen One gawked at The Citizen as she lifted him. She put one of his arms over her shoulder, and they both left through the portal that they came from.

The Chosen One asked, "Do you want to join my team?"

The Citizen said, "No."

PASSAGE #5: THE BIG TALK

The Superhero flew away from another battle against an alien cyborg with spikes. Then on top of one of the skyscrapers, he saw The Citizen waving to him. So, he flew over to him to talk. A few moments later...

The Citizen exclaimed, "YOU OWE ME!!!"

In a panic, The Superhero begged, "I am sorry. Please, forgive me."

The Citizen shouted, "You don't tell, some green-haired woman, my identity and where I live just because you are friends!"

The Superhero said, "Look, the reason why I told her is that she is destined to save the world. She was pretty tense after her journey through your facility and wanted to end it with her getting what she needed. Buuut..."

The Citizen continued, "...I was doing my job. Unlike you and your gal pal, I work for the government. While working, I cannot simply do something nice because it's for a just cause. I must go through paperwork, protocols, and my superiors which I am currently doing for your friend. How about you explain to me why you did this."

As he turned away, The Superhero said, "I think you deserve to learn a little bit about me. Before I became a superhero, I was...I was... a balloonist."

Widening his eyes, The Citizen said, "A... Balloonist?"

Quickly, The Superhero said, "Yes, you don't have to repeat. A yellow energy being attacked me during one of my rides. It shot down my balloon. Luckily, I crashed on top of some trees and climbed down one of the trees, only for the creature to attack me once more. I was unconscious, but when I awoke, I saw her. She said that she destroyed to energy being, but when it was "splattered," its energy infected my body. It granted me the power to generate this energy and use it to augment my body."

The Citizen asked, "So, you got your powers from the remains of an energy creature, and I am guessing that you were thankful for the woman for saving your life."

The Superhero answered, "Yes, she told of her mission and showed me her bluish glow. She inspired me to follow in her footsteps and become a warrior of good. I even manage to change the color of the energy I generate from yellow to blue to represent her and her noble goal."

The Citizen thought to himself that his friend's story might be true. It was also apparent that The

Superhero might be smitten by The Chosen One and was willing to do anything for her. The Chosen One might be trouble down the road, and The Superhero was a powerful asset. If they teamed up, the government would have to face a person who is destined to achieve and a superhuman. The Citizen decided to use *The Big Talk* to protect the government against this eventual outcome and for a bit of payback.

The Citizen said, "Thank you for telling a bit about your origin. I know you told her about where I live because you wanted to aid the one that saved and changed your life."

The Superhero said, "This is true. I wanted to help her as much as I could, and I knew that you would help when you are not working."

The Citizen stated, "That is true about me. Now, If I wanted your help, would you come to my aid, right?"

The Superhero said, "Yes, I would."

Before The Citizen said (Persuasiveness: Probability), "Good, how about the next time I say the code phrase "Gubersocci," you will immediately help me with anything I need for a bit."

The Superhero uttered, "Uh… Yeah. Yes, sure. hehe"

The Citizen said, "That is great to hear. Now, you better keep on making our city safe."

The Superhero replied, "Yeah, it was nice seeing you again."

The Superhero flew off thinking that their argument ended nicely. The Citizen walked to the elevator, thinking about what had just transpired. He hated what he had to do, and he could only assure himself that it was for the good of his country's safety and order as the elevator's door closed.

PASSAGE #6: "JĀNĪ OBU JĀNĪ: ATARASHI JIDAI" EPISODE 1

The Citizen disgruntledly sat on his couch about to watch a show that was a spinoff from his favorite childhood show "Jānī Obu Jānī." A protagonist's story of an endless journey because he keeps forgetting his quest. This led to him having many adventures and meeting many interesting characters you would only meet once and never see again.

The Citizen loved the series because that taught him about grit, holding on to who you are despite the situation. It does not matter how you do your job, just as long it was done the fun way. He was angry because he learned that this spinoff would attract younger viewers with two new main characters. The worst part of it all was that the Protagonist of the first series would be killed off in the first episode.

After the intro to the show, The Citizen watched it with great scrutiny. In a forested path, The Protagonist smiled while swishing his golden-brown hair and brandishing his sword made of a mixture of gold, silver, and bronze. Then, from the view of a crystal ball, a wyvern with an insectoid head watched The Protagonist. The Citizen knew that he was the antagonist of this new series. The Antagonist announced the time to attack, and from shadows behind The Protagonist, gremlins with a glowing knife approached him. The Citizen could not just watch as his hero was about to be ambushed and be gone forever.

As he grabbed the TV, The Citizen screamed (Audibility: Dimension), "Behind You!"

The Protagonist turned around in response to The Citizen's plea. He swiftly slashed all his enemies and turned into black dust. The Antagonist groaned at his nemesis's fortune and turned away to look for more minions.

After looking around, The Protagonist shouted, "Hello! Is there someone here!"

The Citizen decided to try again and replied (A: D), Ahhhhh, Yeah, I am here.

The Protagonist said, "Why can't I see you? Are you a spirit?".

The Citizen said (A: D), "Nonononono, I am no spirit. I am just ahhhhhh..."

Turning away from the TV, The Citizen quickly realized that it could destroy him if he told the truth. So, he decided to make up a new identity. The Citizen turned back to the TV and tried this new power again.

The Citizen said (A: D), "I am a guide of brave souls. I only wish to help you on your newest journey."

The Protagonist said, "I got out of this crazy quest

after killing the King of Paths 3 years ago. I wanted to go on a new journey."

The Citizen said (A: D), "Yes, I have seen a new enemy, and they want to get rid of you. Go down to the meadow and await my instructions."

The Protagonist left for the meadow, and The Citizen sat back to figure out what to do next while the show was on a commercial break. The Citizen was surprised at this development, and he pondered a bit about the ramifications of altering a person's work. This could change The Protagonist's very reality. Then he remembered all the complaints from the real fans of the franchise and how the creator of the show did not want to do it but did not have a choice. The Citizen decided that he was going to keep doing this. He did not wish to see this legendary show become mediocre junk for people who do not know what art meant.

The Citizen said (A: D), "Alright, my man, here is what you need to do now...."

Before he said anything else, the show was taken off the air and replaced with "Technical Difficulties" on the screen. The Citizen may have saved his favorite show's legacy for the moment, but he is sure that they will meet again.

PASSAGE #7: TEAM TRIP- DAY 2

The Citizen sprang out from the tent that he was sleeping in after hearing a scream. He ran out and looked around to check it out. The Scholar jumped out from the other tent, screaming about a centipede touching her. The Citizen sighed with relief.

The Citizen said, "It is not like it was going to kill you or anything."

As she crawled out of the tent, The Heiress said, "Yeah, I thought intellectual types love insects."

Still shaking in a panic, The Scholar uttered, "Not when they are out of a cage crawling under my shirt. When we planned to go on a treasure hunt for team bonding, I thought we would be doing this in the comfort and safety of a mobile laboratory."

After The Citizen and Heiress finished laughing, The trio packed up their campsite to go onward with their quest. They passed through the forest and journeyed up a mountain. The Heiress thought about asking a question to her teammates.

She asked, "Hey guys, Um… Do you have anyone special in mind?"

The Citizen replied, "No."

The Scholar said, "I... am married. That monster indoctrinated my husband. He is just mindless goon now, and I'm trying to come up with a way to free him from his control."

Both of The Scholar's teammates were mortified. The Citizen knows that it would be a difficult task. The Heiress thought this was a sad fate, and she admired her passion and ambition.

The Scholar said to The Citizen, "I believe that you can help break my husband free from his affliction. After all, you did fight a man who said wield the power of "destiny" and won."

The Citizen responded, "I would be happy to help if I can."

The Scholar turned to The Heiress and said, "Anyway, why did you ask us this question?"

Heiress answered, "Uh, you see, I sort of have my eyes on someone."

The Citizen said, "Hmm, you're talking about my friend, the "master" spy."

The Heiress said embarrassingly, "Yes. Do you know anything about him?"

The Citizen said, "Nobody has ever asked me about dating. My brother was the casanova. I was the "cute little brother." A kid too scared to make a single decibel towards a girl. **(He took a deep breath.)** I will give you this tidbit. He is a man who gets into his work. If you want to be under his radar, you must be in his element constantly. It will be long progress, but I believe that your determination and consistency can win him over."

The Heiress said, "Wow, thanks. I am going to try that."

The Citizen said, "No problem."

PASSAGE #8: TEAM TRIP- NIGHT 5

The Citizen stood in front of The Heiress and Scholar, ready to explain his lifestyle upon The Scholar's request. He already told them last night of the general stuff. Tonight, he would disclose more specific information on his lifestyle's power.

The Citizen said, "Alright, team, listen up. As I said last night, The Ridificci Lifestyle's power is to merge one of my attributes with an existential concept. Now, what is considered an existential concept? Simply, it is a concept that humanity had thought up to rationalize how reality works such as time, space, probability, etc."

The Scholar asked, "So, how many existential concepts do you use?"

The Citizen replied, "So far, 7."

The Heiress requested, "Can you show us examples of these powers?"

The Citizen did comply and started with time. He explained that any attribute with time could be random to him. The abilities would be some form of time being delayed, accelerated, slowed down, and even frozen. He looked (Fire Aversion: Time) at the fire, and it quickly went out as if someone used the fast-forward button.

Next, The Citizen explained causality after bringing more firewood. It was simply. It allows him to generate effects or materials based on his attribute. The Citizen reached down and touched (Electricity Affinity: Causality) the firewood. Then a bolt of electricity came out between him and the wood igniting a new fire. The Citizen looked at the empty drinking cup in The Heiress's hand. He went to it and put (Fruit Juice Affinity: Causality) his thumb on it. Juice started to pour out of the space underneath it and into the cup. The Heiress and Scholar were both impressed, but The Citizen explained as the fluid faded away. Whatever manifests only lasts for a few seconds, but the effect that they caused would remain.

Dimensional abilities could either create portals that lead to a realm based on his attribute or interact with this or other realities in unique ways. The Citizen clapped (Loudness: Dimension) his hand and opened a portal that spoke in a loud voice, "**Is this cool or what!?**".

Probability creates events based on the attribute. The Citizen walked up to a tree and grabbed it. He lifted (Strength: Probability) it, and the ground shook. A massive chunk of the earth launched the tree over him, and the tree smashed into two other trees.

Space permitted The Citizen to manipulate the physical space around him to achieve specific effects based on his qualities. The Citizen walked (Speed: Space) right in front of the girls passing several feet and the campfire without seeing him doing it. It can also allow him to summon things from other places. He retook The Heiress's cup and waved (Fruit Juice Affinity: Space) his hand over it. A tiny rift opened up and poured out some juice into it. Unlike his causality abilities, anything that comes out is real and can stay around indefinitely.

Existence allowed The Citizen to manifest any of his attributes into a physical form. The Citizen reached (Dagger Proficiency: Existence) out his right hand, and a yellowish-brown dagger appeared. He threw it at a small rock on the ground, and the knife split it in two. Nothingness is the opposite of Existence. Instead of bringing forth something, it could nullify things or access the power of the void.

The Citizen tossed (Destructiveness: Nothingness) the rock and obliterated it. There was not even a speck of the stone left. The Scholar witnessed the ability with great scientific intrigue, especially since it broke the law of the conservation of mass.

The Heiress uttered, "Yes, Yes. This is fascinating stuff."

The Scholar said, "What an impressive display of some of your arsenal. Tell me, could you learn other concepts?"

The Citizen replied, "Yeah. If you have some suggestions on existential concepts, please let me...

Yawn...know. For now, I am going to hit the floor. Goodnight."

The girls both said, "Goodnight."

PASSAGE #9: THE FINAL DAY OF THE TRIP

The team had finally reached their destination, a temple at a high mountain peak. The Scholar asked The Citizen to go around and place some devices around the temple. The Citizen walked (Multitasking Proficiency: Space) towards the temple. Several more Citizens appeared around the temple to put down the machines. The Heiress brought out a mini- generator for The Scholar to power up her computer and other machinery.

The devices placed around the temple used sonar to make a 3D map of the temple. The Scholar activated the gadgets, and they waited for a while. Soon the route was completed, and The Scholar printed it out. The team looked at it. The Citizen was astonished at the detail of it all, and he could see where all the steps, doorways, and traps were.

The Citizen asked, "Do you two want to go with the temple with me? I do not mind doing this alone. After all, the map shows the prize deep within the mountain. It could take a long time."

The Heiress exclaimed, "Are you kidding me? We've been out here for several days to reach this, and with the real work about to begin, you're giving us a choice to chicken out. Come on, man."

With a smile, The Scholar followed up with, "She's right. We are a team, and this would be an excellent chance to see if our role dynamic can achieve our objective."

The Citizen agreed, and they suited up in dark gray attire. The Heiress wore a backpack with tools like an over- the- shoulder flashlight, explosives, and even a laser made by The Scholar. The Scholar wore a gauntlet with a visual touch screen connected to her computer. They were ready, and they stepped in.

The team walked down the last flight of stairs of the temple. Thanks to the map, the crew avoided most of the traps, but there was one last obstacle, a large door with runes on it. In front of the door, The Citizen moved (Evasiveness: Space) towards it and started to phase halfway through. Then a sphere above glowed, and the door shocked him off.

The Heiress fired a laser at the sphere, and the runes diverted the energy down to the door. Then the whole door glowed and fired the laser right back in a shower of light. The Scholar turned a force field in front of her and The Heiress. The Citizen took (Durability: Existence) the attack head-on with a bronze-colored barrier. Soon, the retaliation dissipated, and the team shut off their defenses. The Citizen was groaning in pain because the shield was only protected from physical damage, but he still felt some of the pain.

The Scholar thought back on how her teammates failed and thought of the solution. She suggested that The Heiress fire the laser once more at the sphere. At the same time, The Citizen should try to send energy through the runes simultaneously. The Citizen stood in front of the door again and waited for The Scholar's signal. After quick "3...2...1.", The Heiress fired her laser again, and The Citizen punched (Electricity Affinity: Causality) rapidly at the door. The Citizen sends massive surges of energy, and, like The Scholar planned, the runes channeled the power to the sphere in the attempt to fire back at him. Before it could do, the laser was already at the orb. The combined energies overloaded the spheroid causing it to shatter.

The door automatically opened with the sphere gone, revealing what they were looking for. It was a pile of scrolls in front of a chute. The walls around the room had pictures that depicted two great forces, forces that The Citizen was very familiar with.

The Heiress asked, "Are these it? I was hoping for some actual treasure because this was our first treasure hunt together."

The Scholar replied, "Oh ho no, these are a lot more valuable than precious materials. These could help me get my husband back and put an end to that madman."

The Citizen chimes in with, "Besides, if you want valuables, the wall pictures are made of what I believe to rubies and sapphires."

The Heiress looked closely at the wall and

squealed to confirm that they were what The Citizen claimed. She started yanking them off the wall one by one with a tremendous passion while The Scholar and The Citizen grabbed all the scrolls. With their destination reached and items in hand and bags, The Citizen asked them to hold on to him. The Citizen breathed (Home Affinity: Space) deeply, and before they even knew what had happened, they were at The Citizen's apartment. He grabbed some refreshments to make a toast for their first big step in being a real team and for their future successes.

PASSAGE #10: PRANKS AT THE PEWS

In great attire, The Citizen rushes (Speed: Causality) through the street, with each step accelerating him to superhuman speed. He overslept because of a mishap from one of The Scholar's experiments. Jumping over people, cars, and even street kiosks, his destination was reached, his church. He made it with a few seconds to spare. Before he could get to the front entrance, an old friend stepped in a way—a man in a dark blue suit and black hair.

He said to The Citizen, "Well, if it isn't the heathen lifestyler."

The Citizen responded, "Can we not do this, *Aemdalis*. We have done this thing every week for three years. I am here because we share the same beliefs."

He uttered, "Says the man who betrays his faith by living a sinful life. If you were truly faithful, you would leave behind your old ways and come back to the righteous path of our faith."

The Citizen said, "Why don't you go to the pews already, you zealot."

The Zealot scoffed and went inside. The Citizen thought that the guy needs to respect a person's life choices or get no respect in return. The Zealot sat at the front aisle like always, and The Citizen sat two pews behind him. Then The Citizen prayed for what he was about to do.

The pianist played the organ, and the churchgoer stood up and sang hymns. The Citizen (Audibility: Space) sang, and his voice was transferred right into The Zealot's ears. He started low and softly, then loud and obnoxiously. The Zealot tried hard not to drop to his knees or scream in pain.

After the songs, the churchgoers walked around shaking hands. While The Zealot was away, The Citizen went to his spot and made (Harming Proficiency: Time) a slapping motion at the air. He left to go to his seat and waited for The Zealot to return. After The Zealot sat down, He felt a powerful, smacking sensation and did not know how it happened. The Citizen chuckled at him.

Soon, the pastor started their sermon, and The Citizen thought one more prank should do it. The Citizen looked (Spying Proficiency: Space) down on his lap, but his sight was moved to the bottom of the pews to see where The Zealot's feet were. He angled his right foot towards his target and stepped (Water Affinity: Space) as water trickled down right underneath The Zealot's shoes. He stepped (Cold Affinity: Causality) again, and the liquid turned to a thin sheet of ice.

The Citizen then started prepping the final phase of the prank. He closed his eyes and thought about the best moments in his life that had to do with warm things. He thought about hot chocolate, the first beam of light of the sun of a new day, and wearing clothes that had just got out of the dryer. The congregation just finished the closing prayer and started to head for the refreshment table. The Zealot stood up, took one step forward, and slipped on the ice. He fell on his rear, and The Citizen touched (Heat Affinity: Causality) the ice on the floor. The ice soon melted into water. The Zealot stood back up and looked at the fluid. As he looked at the water trail, The Citizen moved (Speed: Space) from his spot to the door behind The Zealot that led to the hallway.

The Citizen quickly entered the hallway to avoid being seen by The Zealot. He hid in the bathroom to revel in another victory over his archenemy. Ever since using the Ridificci Lifestyle, most people did not understand him. Still, they soon all accept him except for The Zealot. Even the people in their congregation liked his lifestyle, but he still gave him a hard time. The Citizen was glad that he was not too bright, or he would have already known that it was all The Citizen's fault. He left the bathroom and went to the back exit. Tomorrow, The Citizen will have an important meeting.

The End of Volume 3

VOLUME 4

Published May 22, 2019

PASSAGE #1: INTELLIGENCE MEETING

In a business casual outfit, The Citizen stood before The President and other government officials to discuss a critical issue, The Fated Ones. The Citizen set up his presentation. The President and a woman with a bullet wound scar on her left cheek, the first field marshal in this country's history, whispered to each other as The Citizen finished up.

The Citizen announced, "Ladies and Gentlemen, I am here to report on my findings on the fated ones personally."

The President said, "This must be important since you usually send your reports by other means rather than meeting face-to-face."

As The Field Marshal laughed, she said, "I agree. We barely see you around here. You usually hang around more colorful characters."

After a deep breath, The Citizen continued, "A few months ago, I sent a report about a woman who infiltrated my workplace looking a particular artifact. She got through all the traps that the staff laid before her and got to my office. However, it is not the first time someone managed that feat. What caught my attention was her incredulous claim of being "The

Chosen One" of this world."

The Field Marshal said in a questioning manner, "You mean like the ones in stories and movies?"

The Citizen turned on the projector and said, "Do not take this lightly. I have seen her in action on camera and with my own eyes."

The Citizen showed a short video clip depicting The Chosen One fighting her way through men, women, traps, monsters, and even ghosts. The officials began muttering amongst each other.

The Citizen said, "This Chosen One came to my home after I helped put her away. I couldn't fight her in a public location without risking collateral damage. So, I complied with her demands."

The Field Marshal stood up and yelled, "We do not submit to criminals, especially not one of my...."

The Citizen interrupted, "Field Marshal, please! This might seem to be an act of passiveness, but I needed more data on her before deciding what to do next. So, we chatted. I learned she became the Chosen One recently. She was a mere civilian with no special skills or talents to speak of, but she managed to get through several facilities with nothing but her bare hands. This is very intriguing."

The President said, "So, what made her so capable?"

The Citizen replied, "I am glad you ask. The Chosen One possesses a unique connection to a higher force, which allows her to intensify her physical capabilities and achieve almost any task at will. She might also have the ability to sway people to her side. The girl did this to the superhero in my city, but it gets more interesting. In my last encounter, not only was her fighting prowess improved, but she developed a new ability."

The President said, interrupting The Citizen with a concerned insight, "You mentioned "Fated Ones" awhile back as if there were more than just her out there."

The Citizen said, staring at the President for a moment before answering, "Fortunately, there is only one other. This leads us to the real problem, as you know. The no-name dictator orchestrated the "Princess Crusade." I was at the event, but I did not face him at that time because of .... another reason. Anyway, when I finally infiltrated his fortified stronghold again with an agent of ours, I met him face-to-face. He is a fated one also, but he is also an actual threat. He claimed to be "The Dark One," a man, who is destined rule the world or, so he claims."

An official asked, "Can he do what the other can?"

The Citizen said, "Indeed, but he has his own unique abilities. He can absorb another's "destiny" to strengthen himself and subjugate his victims. In the end, this is not the worst thing about him or his plans for world domination."

Another official asked, "What do you mean by

that?"

The Citizen answered, "We are in a loop."

The Citizen revealed his discovery at the temple his team found. A library of sorts stored the written stories of other fated ones. He had no idea who made the temple but translating the oldest one of these manuscripts revealed that the first fated one came to be over 5000 years ago. The officials mutter amongst themselves again. Finally, one official asked The Citizen what all this was about.

The Citizen summed it up for the group. "Well, it is really about the battle for the future of our world. From what the writing said, if The Chosen One wins, she will bring an age of peace to our world. If The Dark One wins, there would be an age of total servitude. Regardless of who wins when the age slowly ends, a new civilization will replace the old. Then new fated ones would emerge, and the loop would begin again. It is our destiny!"

The President said, "Is there a way to …

The Citizen interrupted, "…to stop it. We are dealing with a force that reshaped this world countless times. You are asking me if I have a plan to spare us from possibly losing everything. I don't think we cannot stop it, but we can minimize the suffering. I suggest we focus our effort on neutralizing the dictator or pushing the final confrontation towards the other Chosen One's favor."

The Field Marshal said, "We cannot show either of them that we are spineless. Remember from your previous report. This woman broke into a government-owned facility. She is as much of a threat in some ways as the dictator. If I didn't know better, I would believe that you have also fallen under her wiles." She stared into The Citizen's eyes in a cold lingering manner.

The Citizen declared, "Don't mistake my logic for treason. If I were with her, I wouldn't be explaining how much trouble we are in. Trust me, I don't want to be anywhere near them, but I am already involved. I already defeated The Dark One once and The Chosen One twice."

The Field Marshal said, "Okay, problem solved. Just go find those two and take them down again."

The Citizen stated, "I am sorry, but I do not have much of a taste for combat nowadays. I will step in when and if the situation becomes dire. Even if my lifestyle can give me the means to harm them, something will just save them. It is fate, remember?"

The President articulated, "If your research says that the fated ones fought each other for years, then there must be some way we could intervene or a way to prevent this ghastly conflict."

"I do, but I wanted to convince you just to let things be. Since you are so impatient, I will tell you another one of my discoveries. In our research, it is revealed that relics of the "mystical" variety could assist us. If we could get a couple of excavation teams to these locations," The Citizen said, pointing at "Xs" on the next screen. "The world might stand a chance against these wielders of fate. I am already part of a team with the sole purpose of taking down The Dark One."

The President declared, "We'll get on finding those artifacts immediately. Since you and your team have a better grasp on this situation, you are tasked with neutralizing one or both fated ones."

The Citizen nodded in agreement to this task.

The President continued, "If our business is finished, this meeting is adjourned."

The officials started to leave while talking to each other about the meeting. After The Citizen gathered his things, The President and Field Marshal came to speak to him.

The President uttered, "That was a nice presentation. You don't usually like talking about serious things without using your lifestyle."

The Citizen said, "Yeah, but you know how those stuffed shirts get when I do something unusual. Plus, it shows that I am serious about this matter. I am going to miss my gig at the facility, but without The Monument, there is no reason to stay."

The President said, "I can make you a special agent. Then you can be more flexible in working on this new mission."

The Citizen said, "I accept your suggestion. I hope being a special agent pays well."

The President said, "You are working directly beneath me. Of course, you'll be paid nicely, and it's not because you are my little brother. You are intelligent, capable, and powerful. You are the right one for this job. It is your destiny."

The Field Marshal expressed remorsefully, "Look, I am sorry for what I said before. I didn't want to believe my own son would betray us."

With a warm smile, The Citizen said, "Apology accepted, Mom. You were right to question my loyalty, and you were in your "Worksona." You just play tough for the people and the troops."

With a long sigh, The Field Marshal said, "Let's not talk about it anymore. Anyway, are you two going to your brother's wedding?"

The President replied, "Of course, I wouldn't miss it for anything."

The Citizen answered, "Eh, I was thinking of … skipping…it."

After a soul-piercing stare, The Field Marshal said, "Look, I know that you are not very fond of these sorts of things, but it would mean a lot to your brother if you showed up. Despite your ages, he looks up to you."

After giving a long sigh, The Citizen said, "Okay,

okay, okay, I'll go."

The President said, "Great, you can even make it a...vacation."

With a slight twitch, The Citizen said, "Yeahhh, and It is going to be my standard month off per year. Plus, I am starting to burn out. I need to get back. My team is going to set up our temporary HQ and want to be there to assist."

The President stated, "Hey Bro, if you see Green Hair again, tell her I will pardon her, but if she gets into government business again, she is just as condemned as her counterpart."

The Citizen said, "Roger that, Sis."

PASSAGE #2: JUST A DREAM

The Citizen floated in the air. Sound asleep. He dreamt a simple dream, and it was the same kind he had since he first gained the Ridificci Lifestyle. He was a stick figure man in a white void, and every time he would hear a voice say to do something. In this dream, a basketball hoop appeared, and a voice said: "Get the ball through the hoop." The Citizen grabbed a ball and threw it, but he missed. He went up to the hoop and scored.

Once again, The Voice said, "Get the ball through the hoop."

The Citizen knew what he had to do in this dream. He had to use his lifestyle to achieve the task until he woke up. He readied himself and knew he had to follow the entire dream sequence to its conclusion.

Round 2- Strength: Existence

The Citizen manifested a powerful aura around his hand to grab the ball from the ground and throw it straight up the air. He waited a minute until the ball went through the hoop with a fiery return velocity.

The Voice said, "Get the ball through the hoop."

Round 3- Rapier Proficiency: Dimension

After The Citizen shoots, the ball hit the backboard and was about to bounce away from the hoop. Then The Citizen waved his hand upward, and a rapier came out of a portal underneath the ring to skewer the ball. The weapon slowly moved down past the circle with the ball.

The Voice said, "Get the ball through the hoop."

Round 4- Accuracy: Time

The ball went into the hoop immediately through a time skip.

The Voice said, "Get the ball through the hoop."

Round 7- Laser Affinity: Causality

The Citizen threw the ball, and he flicked his finger. A small beam fired out and shot the ball, deflating it before reaching the hoop. The laser went through the backboard.

The Voice said, "Get the ball through the hoop."

Round 14- Accuracy: Probability

When The Citizen tossed the ball, the hoop bent downward for the ball to get in and went right in before completely falling over.

The Voice said, "Get the ball through the hoop."

Round 28- Stretchability: Space

The Citizen stretched his arms with the ball, and the space warped around his arm, allowing them to be extended to an unnatural length. He then dunked the ball in the hoop.

The Voice said, "Get the ball through the hoop."

The Citizen readied himself for his next attempt until a flash from his past hit him. He had a brief moment of memory about the scientist who wished to know the meaning of life that he was willing to die for it, and he did. Before this man died, he was told that everything in the universe goes through some form of change and that the process would never stop. The Citizen thought for a minute. Could this information be a source of intervention? Perhaps this information could be helpful.

Once more, The Voice said, "Get the ball through the hoop."

Round 56- Accuracy: Change

A brilliant brown light enveloped The Citizen, and that light sprang forth onto the area, and he...

The Voice said, "Have a Nice Day."

The Citizen woke up with R-shaped pupils wide open. He walked his way to the bathroom to get his contact lens and put them on to allow him to see once more. He thought about what he had dreamt about last night but soon forgot most of it. It felt like this dream was significant for some reason, but why?

PASSAGE #3: THE EXPLORER AND THE REVIVED KINGDOM OF ILLECELUCUU

The Citizen, The Scholar, and The Heiress walked down a street that led to a museum. The Citizen wanted to ask his father, a great explorer, to help excavate the relics. He might be a good treasure hunter, but his father made treasure hunting an art form.

The Scholar asked The Citizen, "So, your father was the one who gave you the map that led you to that orb. Where did he find it?"

The Citizen said, "I will tell you what my dad told me."

The Citizen told (Imaginativeness: Existence) them that it started way before The Citizen was even born. A ray of light rose out of his hand and displayed a small image. It showed The Explorer, young and robust, discovering a map etched behind a wall in a motte-style castle. That map would lead him to a hidden, ancient society.

From that castle, he traveled east until reaching a mountain range. The Explorer reached the top of one of the mountains to see nothing but dense fog. He went down into the mist and started to lose consciousness. This fog must be poisonous because he saw skulls just below him.

The Explorer's eyes shut with the last things on his mind were his wife and his daughter. He woke up to some noise in a dark cave. A dark hand reached out for him and poked on his left cheek. The Explorer collapsed once more before he awakened to someplace new, a town being managed by knights. The knights were carrying him to their king. The townspeople just stared at him, wondering who this man was.

The Explorer thought he went back into Medieval times. They reached the castle in the center of the town, which appeared to be a tall spire with four other towers protruding at its top. The knights dragged him into the building. After a minute, They reached the throne room, and The King sat with a firm look on his face. His queen seated beside him. The Explorer made a nervous gulp and waited for his fate.

The King welcomed The Explorer to the Kingdom of Illecelucuu and asked him why he was in their secret society. The Explorer honestly told him that he followed a map to this place, and The King understood what he was talking about.

To make a long history short, their ancestors made ancient, terraforming, wish-fulfilling technology. One group did not want to use them and plunged into civil war with those who tried to use them. They lost and were exiled, but not before stealing those devices. The exiled hid the devices and lived in another kingdom in the west. Thousands of years later, the descendants of the victors searched for the descendants of the exiles to bring them back to Illecelucuu for the sole purpose of repopulating their people. They went back with them and saved their culture. The exile descendants also brought back the culture they were born into, hence why today's Illecelucian culture has a similar aesthetic to the Dark Ages. The map was there to show the stragglers where they went. There was a message in their old language to help them avoid the miasma.

The Explorer told The King of the realm what happened to the world. They should not be hidden beneath a cloud of poison. He could help them reconnect with the rest of the world, and in turn, they could assist the world with their advances. Before The Explorer could continue, The King noticed the mark on his cheek. The dot began to grow, expand, and burst outward, attacking everyone around The Explorer.

Everyone was restrained. The slate-colored substance quickly crept up a stairway next to the throne. The sound of a machine turning off echoed across the grand hall, and all the Illecelucians panicked. Soon, they all listened to the screams of the villagers from the town. They heard the front door being broken down by something powerful. More of that material emerged from the dark hallway. The Queen cried out that it is the "Darkest Weapon, The Ruinous Lady, Ermmm." The substance grew over her mouth before she could say anything else.

This Ruinous Lady appeared as a young woman with dark gray skin and hair. The substance was wrapped around her like a dress. The Explorer also noticed that the material was on everybody except him and coming from her hair. She strolled by The Explorer and began dealing with some of the knights, and she had them encased with her sinister matter. The King shouted to all who could respond to climb the stairs and turn the machine back on again.

The Explorer ran towards the stairway until The Ruinous Lady swiftly appeared in front of him. He fired at her head with his pistol, but she oozed out more of that material instead of brain and blood. The Ruinous Lady reformed her head, but her target maneuvered over her. The Explorer ran up the stairs because his life depended on it. He prepared a grenade when he saw the end of the stairs.

As predicted, The Ruinous Lady manifested instantaneously from the ooze already there. The Explorer ran right into her and rammed the grenade right in her fluidlike body. He twirled around her to reach for the machine, and before his enemy could do something, the explosive went off, destroying her form. The Explorer activated the device with a lever pull, and it released an energy pulse that pushed the ruinous matter out of the castle and the town below.

The Explorer went down to find that everyone was alright and profusely apologized for what he caused. The King knew it was his fault that they were almost killed, but he saw The Explorer's bravery, resourcefulness, and honesty as genuinely remarkable. He told The Explorer as punishment he would help fix any damage The Ruinous Lady caused, and... to be an ambassador for the outside world. The Explorer agreed. So, The King gave him two rewards for technically defeating her. The Explorer was given full citizenship and his family to the kingdom and some items from their treasure vault.

The Citizen concluded, "My Dad found a lot in their treasury, but the one that caught his eyes was the map which he gave me years later."

From a distance, A man with gray frame glasses shouted, "Hey, if it isn't my big wrecking ball."

The Citizen shouted, "Hey Dad, I have a proposition for you."

PASSAGE #4: THE CHOSEN ONE & THE MUTANT VS THE FIELD MARSHAL & THE CITIZEN

The Chosen One ran down a hallway with a rather large, monstrous man with a large jaw, two talon limbs, and rough, purplish skin. The alarm sounded, and the speaker said to be on the lookout for the mutant that had recently escaped. The pair were about to reach the exit across a big lobby. The Citizen rose through the floor and stood before the entrance as shutters descended to block the door. The Mutant ran ahead of The Chosen One to charge at him. The Citizen raised (Hatchet Proficiency: Existence) his hand, and his weapon emerged as he was ready to swing it down. The Mutant's speed increased enough to knock the hatchet out his hand and shove The Citizen against the glass door. The glass cracked, and The Citizen was pinned.

After a short chuckle, The Mutant said, "This is the last line of defense, some dude with a fancy ax."

The Citizen said, "Oh, I am just stalling my aggressive amigo and…."

The hatchet flew at The Mutant and slashed his

arm. The Mutant roared and stepped away from The Citizen. The Chosen One ran next to The Mutant, ready to defend him.

The Citizen continued, "You did not know that I can control that "Fancy Ax" remotely."

The Chosen One exclaimed, "What are you even doing here? Don't you work in another government facility?"

The Citizen replied, "I am reassigned. Now, I have my new job and a new mission: to stop you and your counterpart. Of course, I do not have to. Listen, The President herself told me that she had pardoned you for your past transgresses, and I can get her to pardon you for what you are doing now if you are willing to relinquish him into my custody. If you continue down this path, then you will be considered a threat, and I get the first crack at you before anyone else."

The Chosen One paused for a moment and thought of her previous fights with The Citizen. She knew that he was tough, and he even harmed a man who took down 30 soldiers. She turned to look at The Mutant as he cradled his wounded arm. She started to doubt herself, and her body trembled. She even slowly stepped back as if her body was ready to run, but she knew there was no turning back now.

It was either give up a friend destined to help her and her quest to save the world ends or become an enemy of the country and fight The Citizen now. The Chosen One looked deep into herself and remembered a time in her past. As a little girl, she let a kid get bullied by other kids. She could have done something, but she would be the target of bullying as well. So, it escalated to the point that the kid who was being bullied got into an unfortunate accident. She could have prevented it, but she was too scared. The Chosen One thought that she had power now. She can do something this time. She then imagined those cruel kids in front of The Citizen, and together, they made a terrifying, shadowy image. She looked at The Mutant and saw the kid in her flashback next to him. The Chosen One's blue aura came forth with blinding intensity.

The Chosen One uttered, "I do not care if I become your enemy. I am not going to let them have their way with him."

With a sigh, The Citizen asked, "Is this your actual choice, *Incomiber*. I understand that you are the "good guy," but I am not going to let you do whatever you want, like breaking out a dangerously unstable man."

The Mutant yelled, "Ever since I was born, I was a test subject. First by my parents, by mad scientists, by occultists, and when the military saved me, I still became a guinea pig."

The Citizen said, "Look, I can help you get out of this mess?"

The Mutant said, "Yeah, but I am sick of talking to another federal ******."

The Chosen One said, "You're right. We need to get out. My friends are waiting outside."

The two rushed at The Citizen, but before they could attack, the ground shook with such a force that it nearly knocked everyone to the ground. Suddenly, a giant mechanical arm rose from the ground, and the rest of it followed. It was The Field Marshal piloting a giant mech in the shape of a demon. She laughed with excitement as The Chosen One and The Mutant just stared in fear as their problem only intensified to unheard levels.

The Field Marshal said, "I can't believe I finally get to use this. So, this is the runt of a woman who my son said is going to be a problem."

The Mutant uttered, "The real monster emerged from her underworld. I'll see to it you get what you deserve."

The Citizen stated, "I tried to convince them, but they made their choice. Just...Just do not go overboard."

The Field Marshal exclaimed, "I'm sorry, but I made sure these weapons are designed for one thing; Pure, Bloody Combat!"

The Field Marshal fired her flamethrower at the duo, and they avoided it with The Chosen One and The Mutant in opposite directions. The Citizen jumped (Speed: Space) right in front of The Mutant and grabbed (Ice Affinity: Causality) his right leg. The Mutant's leg was covered in ice, and he screamed a blood-curdling scream. The Chosen One ran to the rescue, but The Field Marshal finally got her mech out of the ground.

The Field Marshal grabbed The Chosen One and started to electrocute her. After The Chosen One fell into unconsciousness, The Field Marshal let her go and moved to The Citizen and The Mutant. The Chosen One quickly came to and used her destiny power to generate a blue battering ram to attack. She bashed The Field Marshal towards The Citizen, and The Citizen ran out of the way as The Field Marshal continued moving until she hit a wall. The Citizen saw The Chosen One on the move. He pulled (Speed: Space) back his right leg and kicked The Chosen One in the stomach from out of nowhere.

The ice on The Mutant's leg vanished, but The Field Marshal attacked him with a big arm swing. The Mutant got back up and tried to attack, but The Field Marshal slammed him, once again, with a mighty, metallic fist. Then she activated the taser again, and The Mutant also fell unconscious. After that, The Field Marshal turned to her next victim and rocketed towards the other battle.

After avoiding his mother's attack, The Citizen said, "Not again."

With a twisted smile, The Field Marshal bellowed to The Chosen One, "HaaaahahahahGehhaha, this is what your life has led to! Being a test dummy to my newest masterpiece, and you will die knowing that when you mess with a dragon's chick, you get scorched."

The Chosen One made a wall to block more attacks, but The Citizen was right behind her. The Citizen put her in an armlock, and her barrier faded. The Field Marshal raised her mech's arm, and The Citizen pulled back before her attack missed.

The Chosen One asked, "What is going on with her?"

The Citizen replied, "She gets easily worked up in any conflict. This is why she's the Field Marshal. It's safer to receive orders from her than to let her be on the battlefield. So, I need to end this and calm her down before she starts swearing."

The Citizen squeezed (Electricity Affinity: Causality) The Chosen One's arm and shocked her until she passed out again. The Field Marshal stood in front of them, panting like a dog ready to strike.

The Field Marshal snarled, "That was my target!"

The Citizen said, "It is over, mother. She is down. The other is…."

The Mutant grabbed The Field Marshal's mech by the leg and swung it at The Citizen with all his might. The Citizen dropped The Chosen One and raised (Durability: Existence) his arm, as a brownish barrier appeared around him, protecting him from the impact. Unfortunately, the blow was intense enough to make

The Citizen pass out, and The Field Marshal's seatbelt got jammed, so she could not get out. The Mutant grabbed The Chosen One and walked out the door. The Field Marshal screamed with anger and profanity at this defeat while The Citizen still conked out.

PASSAGE #5: A VISIT FROM THE MERITORIOUS KNIGHT

The Citizen finished his breakfast and headed towards his bedroom, still recovering from his last fight with The Chosen One. Before he could make it to the bedroom, there was a knock at the front door. After the door opened, a man stood in front of him. He was tall, bronzed, and handsome. He had a sharp-looking beard that was glorious compared to The Citizen's fuzz. He was practically elated to see him, while The Citizen, on the other hand, was somewhat dismayed towards him.

The man exclaimed, "How are you doing, brother!"

With a sigh, The Citizen said, "Well, if it isn't The Meritorious Knight. What are you doing here and so far away from your beloved betrothed?"

THE MERITORIOUS KNIGHT answered, "I am just getting some junk out of our folks' place and hope to ask my little monster man a favor."

The Citizen said, "Which would be?"

THE MERITORIOUS KNIGHT said, "I want you to fight me using the powers of a Thunderbird."

With a groan, The Citizen said, "Really, I just recovered from a fight. I don't want to fight one of Illecelucuu's greatest knights right now."

THE MERITORIOUS KNIGHT cried out, "Come on, little brother. I am going on a quest to slay one, and I know that you have seen at least one at your "zoo." So, you know what it is capable of, and for the record, you are also one of Illecelucuu's greatest knights."

The Citizen said, "I am not a knight. I just wore that armor one time for my protection. Anyway, I... I will help prep you, but first, we will need to go somewhere."

A while later, the brothers were in a big, white room. The Scholar and Heiress looked through a window to see more of The Citizen's fighting style. He recollected what he learned about the thunderbird species and how they fight. Then he looked at the large, bulbous ceiling lamps and thought it would be the perfect vantage point.

The Citizen spoke, "Since, You are going to fight a Thunderbird. The first thing you need to know is...."

The Citizen bent his knees and jumped (Thunderbird's Lightning Affinity: Causality) with a powerful flash of blue lightning with a brownish hue. The Citizen vanished, and the electricity he left behind caused the whole room to go dark with only the light from the girls' viewing room shining on THE MERITORIOUS KNIGHT.

On a ceiling lamp, The Citizen continued, "... they only appear in the darkest and most violent storms. The second thing is that they aren't ashamed of striking an unaware prey."

The Citizen fired (TLA: C) a shower of punches that created bolts of lightning that looked like feathers. The Citizen's attack struck THE MERITORIOUS KNIGHT, but a bright, golden glow rose out from where THE MERITORIOUS KNIGHT stood. THE MERITORIOUS KNIGHT, wearing golden armor, jumped right at The Citizen with high speed out of the light.

Through his falcon-esque helmet, THE MERITORIOUS KNIGHT uttered, "Haha, truly this be a battle to remmm...."

Before finishing his sentence, The Citizen kicked (TLA: C) THE MERITORIOUS KNIGHT and released another supernatural bolt. THE MERITORIOUS KNIGHT fell (Thunderbird Affinity: Existence) towards the ground, and the head and a wing of thunderbird effigy emerged from The Citizen's back. As THE MERITORIOUS KNIGHT hits the floor, The Citizen, using the manifestation, flew around in the air readying his next attack. THE MERITORIOUS KNIGHT stood up and watched his brother flying around like a firefly doing a figure 8. He thought that since The Citizen was no longer stationary, he was going for a direct attack. His little brother was behind him in a flash and threw the effigy at him. The thing pecked and scratched him, but THE MERITORIOUS KNIGHT's armor protected him. THE MERITORIOUS KNIGHT let loose a brilliant blast to dissipate the effigy and charged at the now defenseless brother.

The Citizen said, "I think that should be enough."

Still charging, THE MERITORIOUS KNIGHT uttered, "No way, I am a knight. I fight for honor and the art of combat to sharpen my skills. If I can defeat a monster like you, then the king and queen can finally have faith in me!"

THE MERITORIOUS KNIGHT's right arm shined with intense mystical power. He jumped in the air to land one mighty blow, and The Citizen swiftly assaulted (Plasma Affinity: Causality) THE MERITORIOUS KNIGHT with a slash attack forged from red hot matter. The attack knocked THE MERITORIOUS KNIGHT away from The Citizen.

The Citizen demanded, "This. Battle. Is. Over. You got what you needed. So, can I please go back home and get some rest?"

The Meritorious Knight nodded to agree, and his brother left the room. The Citizen told the girls that he would come in tomorrow to discuss their new assignment and walked (Home Affinity: Space) away until he vanished.

The Heiress said, "Why did you call your brother a monster?"

As he walked out, The Meritorious Knight explained in a solemn and sincere tone, "Don't get me wrong, I love him, and he is a good man and brother. It's just something I joke around with, but sometimes, he can be too powerful to be seen as a person instead of something mystical and dangerous."

After The Meritorious Knight left, The Heiress and The Scholar stared at each other and thought about his word.

PASSAGE #6: THE DARK ONE'S DARK SECRET

The Citizen and his teammates stood on a cliff overseeing The Dark One's new HQ, another castle with no forcefield. The Citizen planned to go in alone to see what he was doing now. The Scholar equipped him with a camera, and The Heiress wielded a rocket launcher, and she was prepared to use it when The Citizen needed to escape or to cause some severe damage when he did get away.

The Citizen jumped (Wind Affinity: Probability) in the air, and a powerful gust of wind propelled him and almost his teammates even further up. He shortly fell towards the castle's battlement. The Citizen landed (Durability: Nothingness), face first without any unfortunate results except extreme pain. Without any physical damage, the pain quickly subsided.

He went down the stairs and began his mission. He walked (Evasiveness: Dimension) through a hallway while in a different dimensional field. He passed through some guards without ever seeing him.

Then The Citizen wandered into a room with blue lights, and it was a lab with something in a giant glass cube at the end. He went closer to see that it was a creature surrounded by a blue liquid. The Creature stood over 8 feet tall and looked like a reptilian feline. Its limbs were extremely muscular, and its scales looked like bladed armor; it would mean it was made to be quite a dangerous predator. The Citizen looked up and saw some writing that said, "Project: Chosen Chaser."

The Scholar said to look at the controls next to The Creature's container through the communicator, and The Citizen turned it on and read that it was precisely what it was. It is a genetically manufactured animal meant to hunt down The Chosen One and her allies. Through extensive research on The Dark One's own "Destiny Energy," they managed to give The Creature the ability to locate anything with The Chosen One's destiny energy signature, which they obtained through long-distance observation and sample gathering.

To his teammates, The Citizen said, "I think we can use it against its creators."

The Scholar explained, "Maybe you're right. If this control unit help regulates it, we can reprogram it. Okay, follow my instruction...."

The Citizen grabbed (The Scholar Affinity: Space) the air and pulled out The Scholar halfway through a rift. He thought this was much easier. After regaining some composure from what The Citizen did, The Scholar put some hidden subroutines into The Creature's programming. As she finished, The Creature thrashed around in response and eventually stopped.

To complete this little sabotage, The Citizen found what appeared to be a cylinder containing The Dark One's "Destiny Energy," and The Scholar analyzed it so that The Creature can now track down The Dark One, not just The Chosen One.

He turned off the computer, and The Scholar disappeared as two scientists walked in. The Citizen hid behind the control unit. Luckily, they did not notice. The Citizen left (Evasiveness: Dimension) the lab and decided to leave. He went back to the battlement that he landed, but The Dark One was there with one of his nameless subordinates this time. The Citizen stayed hidden with his ability still active and listened in.

The Dark One spoke, "There are times I wonder why I am fated to do this. Then I remember that I tried to deviate from my path, but I always wind up back on this course. When I was young, I tried to have a life as an owner of a bakery, believe it or not. It burned down because the oven inexplicably exploded. Then I created a small charity that grew to a nationwide organization until a corrupted sect took it over. They used my organization as a vantage point to distribute drugs. I wanted to shut it down, but the money was too good. I reported the sect to the authorities and kept to drug trading with all its revenue going to myself."

The Dark One continued, "2 years ago, I left all that behind when I met the most intriguing young woman in my life. She taught me about living life, taking in every experience as food for the soul, and being who I want to be. I married her within the first month I met her. We were delighted to be together, but one night...."

The Citizen witnessed The Dark One shed a tear from a distance, and then one became a sorrowful stream. The Dark One cried out the name of his wife and wailed that he was sorry. With a morbid look on his face, The Citizen overheard the fate of The Dark One's wife. After The Dark One's outburst, He turned to his minion and thanked him for listening to his tale. Before his minion could reply, The Dark One blasted him into dust, with red energy, stating that his past must remain in the darkness, and he left, passing The Citizen still under his power's effect.

The Citizen ran (Speed: Space) off the battlement and teleported about a mile away from the castle, gasping for breath. He headed back to his teammates and discussed what he saw, and The Dark One's story also mortified them. When The Citizen returned, The Heiress fired her rocket launcher at the castle, and the team walked away under cover of darkness, leaving items that would make The Dark One think it was The Chosen One who attacked him.

PASSAGE #7:
MUSIC-MAKING

The Citizen sat on his couch in his apartment room thinking about what he would do on his vacation at Illecelucuu. He recently had a chat with his brother about the many festivities held there. One of these events was a talent competition.

He wondered what he could do. Maybe he could just show some new abilities, but the Illecelucian know him and his lifestyle. It would just be general amazement and not the kind of amazement found in a true spectacle. It should be something like a well-scripted play or an orchestra. That is when it hit The Citizen. He tapped (Music Affinity: Causality) the armrest, and a weak piano sound came out.

The Citizen decided to be a one-person band at the talent competition, but he was not really into music. So, utilizing this affinity would be almost useless. He decided it was time to get musical. The Citizen walked outside his apartment and listened for music his power would bring forth. Unfortunately, there was nothing outside but beeping cars and loud construction. So, he went back inside and went on his computer.

He looked up what makes music the way it is. In

scientific terms, multiple sounds are put together in a unique pattern. The Citizen tapped the desktop once to make a sound and did it two more times. Together, those weak sounds made better reverberation. After a while, The Citizen decided that he might not create a symphony with one tap of the finger yet, but he might have something with some dynamic movement and dancing.

Music was art manifested from the artist's soul on an artistic level. What genre should represent The Citizen's soul? Heavy Metal, Country, Dubstep, or maybe a remix version of Illecelucian melody. The Citizen reminisced (Memory Proficiency: Existence) about some of the songs from Illecelucuu, and an energy-based mass emerged from him. It made images of The Citizen's memories. It showed horns and nothing but horns. So, he scrapped the ideas. He decided just to experiment until he found a sound that he liked.

The Citizen made sounds and music throughout the night and into the morning. Before he could collapse from exhaustion, there was light knocking at the door. The Citizen stumbled to it and hoped it wasn't The Chosen One or brother again. It was his landlord, a very timid little man. He said that he heard from other tenants about loud noises.

The Citizen apologized and said that he found the sound he was looking for anyway. The Landlord was relieved and walked down the hall and knocked on another door with vigor and intensity. The tenant opened the door, and The Landlord let them have it with harsh words about evicting them if they forgot to pay rent again. Then he stormed off in a huff, and The Citizen always wondered why he never treated him like that.

PASSAGE #8: REDESIGN

The Citizen ran down a tunnel of a cave leading into a cavern. On top of a ledge was a man wearing nothing but a loincloth ripping and sewing fur coats with crazy speed. The Citizen shouted at him, and the man noticed him.

The Citizen yelled, "Where is Mercdith, Skinwalker!?"

The Skinwalker said, "Oh, the Wapaloosie pelt. Here, You can have what's left."

The Skinwalker threw down a sleeve and some remnants to the ground, and they continued moving around. The Citizen was relieved and furious. The Skinwalker revealed his masterpiece, a cloak made of all the coats and pelts he made years ago.

The Skinwalker exclaimed, "Hahahaha, Yes. With this cloak, I will be the most powerful animal in the world. I never thought about it until a few months ago. used my power to steal and cause mischief, but now, I will use this new form to conquer the land."

The Skinwalker put on the hood, and he morphed into a massive beast with dark vermilion fur. His body changed into something like a mountain lion. Spikes grew out from his back and tail, and sword-like claws spouted out his paws. He produced long fangs that could make even male walruses jealous. Then The Skinwalker let loose a roar that shook the cavern and licked his chops at his first prey.

The Skinwalker pounced (Evasiveness: Space) at a frightened Citizen. The Citizen raised his right fist at him with his eyes closed, and The Skinwalker went for his prey. As the beast lands, he almost falls over because he went through him. The Skinwalker's eyes were getting heavy, and his limbs were too weak to support his immense body, and he collapsed to the ground. The Citizen walked to him with a calmer demeanor than before.

The Skinwalker whimpered, "What...what diiid yoouuu doOoOo?"

The Citizen explained, "I have some experience dealing with supernatural animals, and your plan of attack was too obvious. If you want to be an animal, I will treat you like one. I had a tranquilizer dart in my hand when you went right through me."

The Skinwalker roared in defeat as his eyes closed and he reverted to his human form. The Citizen took off the cloak, balled it up, and threw it in the air. He shot (Fire Affinity: Causality) a tiny fireball at the fur coat burst into flame and came down as ash. The Citizen reached (Evasiveness: Space) for The Skinwalker and phased through his body to pull out the dart. He carried him out and took him to the proper authorities.

Later, The Citizen went to many tailors in the

hope of making a new jacket with the offcuts of Meredith, but none of them wanted to work on a pelt that kept on moving. The Citizen went to The Heiress to see if she knew someone who could help. The Scholar overheard their conversation and volunteered to uptake this venture. She always wanted to learn new crafts and got a lot of books and fabrics.

Days passed; The Citizen received a call from The Scholar that she had finished the jacket. The Citizen (Speed: Space) ran into a portal and appeared before The Scholar. After the initial shock, The Scholar revealed the new apparel. It was a dark gold-colored hoodie with black circles on the shoulders and his mark on the back.

With joy, The Citizen said, "Oh, Thank you. This is so cool. I love it, and it looks very slimming."

The Scholar said, "I appreciate those comments, but since this has less of the Wapaloosie material in this one, it won't be able to carry you or anyone else. It can still move around by itself, though."

The Citizen said, "I don't care. "

The Citizen put on the jacket and smiled that he had a new look. That and no one would mistake him for an escaped animal. The Citizen shook his friend's hand vigorously and left quickly to strut with his new threads.

PASSAGE# 9: LET'S TALK ABOUT YOU

The Citizen's psychiatrist called him to come to his office. The Citizen got there and talked to the receptionist, and she said that the psychiatrist was ready for him. The Citizen jumped (Wind Affinity: Causality:) and flew (Evasiveness: Space) right through the ceiling. The Citizen knocked on the door to The Shrink's office, and he was told to come in.

After opening a door, The Citizen said, "Hey, Doc."

The Shrink responded, "Oh, Hello, my boy. Come in."

The Citizen asked, "What is this about?"

The Shrink answered, "I received a call from your pastor. That you are pranking one of your fellow churchgoers...again."

The Citizen argued, "Oh C'mon, He deserved it. He keeps on trying to put me down, although we both follow the same religion. That guy is just jealous ever since military school. I dare even say that he only came to my church to see if I turned the congregation into an...occult or something. So, then he can prove that I am a monster, ship me off to space, and blow up that ship when I least expect it."

The Shrink said, "You're over exaggerating. Look, you need to stop giving into this...this mischievous side of yours."

"Look (Malleability: Existence)," said The Citizen twisting and bending some ethereal material, "I don't have a mischievous side. It's just my sense of justice is pettier than righteous at times. If someone does you wrong, do you wish you could give them some payback?"

The Shrink replied, "I know, I know, but you still shouldn't use your power like that."

The Citizen said, "How should I use my lifestyle? The last time I check, there are no laws when it comes to bending reality to your whim. The last thing my master said before I left the metaphysical realm was, and I quote, "Do what you will." Frankly, I am doing pretty well. The world is still spinning, and it isn't exploding. So, we should drop this whole "powers" thing for now."

The Shrink said, "Very well, Let's talk about something that your mother and sister talk to me about, The Fated Ones."

The Citizen whined, "Oghhhh, Why do we need to talk about that? Should this be top secret stuff?"

The Shrink said, "You forget I am a government-sanctioned psychiatrist, and they want to make sure that you don't get too involved in this matter."

The Citizen said, "I am not going to go crazy like mom did when one of them broke out a biologically unstable man. I am not like her."

The Shrink stated, "You might not go mad the way your mother gets but the threat of you becoming berserk is much bigger than either of those two. You would be worse off than your cousi...."

The Citizen hollered, "We are not here to talk about your mistake!"

The two just looked at each other while trying to regain their poise. The Citizen brought a chair to The Shrink's desk, sat down, and cleared his throat. The Shrink cleared his throat as well.

The Citizen said, "I...did not mean to say that, but it is like I told you I am not like my mother. I will not be like that, especially since this is serious. How can I find any fun with fighting?"

The Shrink voiced, "Okay, I believe you, but if you do feel that mindset, do you remember your exercise?"

The Citizen replied, "Yes, I remember."

The Shrink asked, "Good. Now, how's your dating life?"

The Citizen expressed, "Uhhhhhggggggggg!"

PASSAGE# 10: THE EXPEDITION (PART 1)

The Citizen looked at a board in his apartment with lots of data and pictures of unusual creatures. He looked away and picked up a backpack filled to the brim with gear. Walking towards the door, The Citizen took a deep breath and opened it. In front of him, THE MERITORIOUS KNIGHT stood tall.

After another deep breath, The Citizen said with a smile, "Oh, Hello brother, what you are doing here?"

THE MERITORIOUS KNIGHT answered, "Ha, I am glad to see you with a sunnier disposition, but I was here to see if we could hang out before I head back to Illecelucuu."

The Citizen said, "That would be great, but I have something else planned, my Phantom Beast Expedition. My research may have helped me triangulate where they might appear next."

THE MERITORIOUS KNIGHT inquired, "What is a Phantom Beast?"

The Citizen explained that not much is known about them, but he surmised that they exist both in the physical and metaphysical worlds. They are elusive and are said to be powerful. The Citizen wanted to see these creatures, document them, and add their power to his repertoire of abilities.

THE MERITORIOUS KNIGHT said, "Hmm, That sounds like a great outing for us, brothers."

The Citizen exclaimed, "Oh, I aaaah... I kind of made this a "me time" thing. Besides, I only got only enough supplies for one."

THE MERITORIOUS KNIGHT said, "It will be special now we can share this experience. Plus, I know you have some power just to make enough supplies. So, just do it already."

After taking an even deeper breath, The Citizen agreed that he could come if he did nothing to ruin this. He grabbed another bag from his closet and opened (Memory Proficiency: Dimension) it. A portal opened and poured out items from his memories of what he needed for this trip into the bag. With the pack filled, the two left to begin their journey. The brothers soon were riding on a train, with The Citizen in a luxury coach and THE MERITORIOUS KNIGHT in regular coach a few cars down.

The Citizen snoozed soundly. Meanwhile, THE MERITORIOUS KNIGHT grumbled to himself about how he had to pay for his ticket. At the end of the train, a grayish speck moved around through crates. Trainman entered the last car trying to find something, but instead, something found him. The glop soon ran through the cars until it reached THE MERITORIOUS KNIGHT's car. It crawled up the ceiling and grew an eye to send an evil look at who it was after. It continued to the coupling and destroyed it by crushing it with great force. This separated the cars from the rest of the train as the slime kept on moving.

The train reached its destination late afternoon, and The Citizen woke up to get off. When he got out, he saw many people talking about some of the cars missing. One of them had been the one his brother was riding. He decided to find him but felt a hand gently holding onto his arm. The Citizen turned to see something he hoped never to witness. The Ruinous Lady was standing behind him. Despite appearing as a young woman, it was like being held by a strong adult man. Her calm, almost doll-like demeanor chilled The Citizen right down to his core.

The Citizen asked with a grunt, "What you are doing here? This is not Illecelucuu."

The Ruinous Lady replied, "Rebel culture was detected outside of rebel base."

The Citizen utter, "Just grand, It was a while ago I mentioned you, and now you are here. My guess, you are here to make sure I don't get in the way of what you have cooked up for my brother."

The Ruinous Lady replied, "Correct, the rebel ally might pose a threat to the mission to eliminate the other rebel and his technology. Since former rebel ally does not possess any rebel technology, no harm will fall on rebel ally unless they resist."

With another grunt, The Citizen muttered, "Man, you sure like to say "Rebel" a lot. In other words, like a robot, you cannot completely deviate from your programming to eliminate anything that relates to Illecelucians, who rebelled against your creators. Anyway, you won't attack me unless I attack or try to resist your attempt to confine me here."

The Ruinous Lady replied, "Correct."

After taking the deepest breath in the last 6 hours, The Citizen said (Multitasking Proficiency: Space), "Well then, there are over a thousand ways to get out this...."

From behind The Citizen, Another Citizen said, "...And chose this one just to mess with you."

The Ruinous Lady grabbed the other Citizen, and then another showed up to be seized by her new appendage. Then a whole bunch appeared until The Ruinous Lady couldn't keep track of them all. Since all of them are being submissively captured by her generated tendrils, she cannot use brute force, just restraining methods only. Then one of The Citizens managed to get outside her range and ran back to help his brother.

As he left, The Citizen exclaimed, "You were made to beat Illecelucian Knights, but you cannot beat me with all my tricks."

End of Volume 4

VOLUME 5

Published September 19, 2019

PASSAGE #1: THE EXPEDITION (PART 2)

The Citizen walked across the vast plains to find his brother's train car. Before taking another step, he saw what the other Citizens could see. He saw himself from behind. The Ruinous Lady descended from the sky with many Citizens still wrapped around in her appendages. They all screamed at him to keep running. The Citizen shrieked and ran from the elongated tendrils. He duplicated himself once more to elude his pursuer again hopefully.

Soon, The Citizen was feeling dizzy. There were too many of him, and he could not focus. So, all The Citizens faded until there was one outside The Ruinous Lady's grasp. The Citizen ran (Speed: Space) and vanished before being caught. Miles away, The Citizen hid behind a big rock before seeing The Ruinous Lady swirling around in the air in an amorphous form. The Citizen realized he could just teleport to his brother.

The Citizen jumped (Brother Affinity: Space) and appeared next to THE MERITORIOUS KNIGHT, who had only been a jump away. Both of them were almost crushed by a tail from a gray wyvern. THE MERITORIOUS KNIGHT's armor glowed as he jumped toward the beast sending it flying with one punch. The wyvern flew back around to continue its assault.

The Citizen asked, "Where are the other passengers who were with you."

As THE MERITORIOUS KNIGHT pointed in a far-off direction, he answered, "They left to go to the nearby town."

As he grabbed his brother, The Citizen said, "Good, we're leaving."

THE MERITORIOUS KNIGHT exclaimed, "But, but we cannot leave. There is a vicious creature on the loose."

The Citizen stated, "Look, you wanted to come on my expedition. So, we are doing this my way."

The wyvern flew (Fleeing Proficiency: Space) straight at them, but the two disappeared. It morphed itself into a giant sphere, and more ruinous matter merged with it before slowly moving away from the area to its following location. Later on, night had fallen on a clear lake, and the two brothers sat behind some bushes.

THE MERITORIOUS KNIGHT scolded The Citizen, "We should have stayed and fought that thing."

The Citizen said, "That thing was The Ruinous Lady. She is LITERALLY only here because of you. Now, hush. They should be arriving...now."

At the lake's center, spectral entities started to appear from nowhere. The Citizen smiled widely as his research had finally begun to bear fruit. The phantom beasts were shapeless and somewhat translucent in appearance until limbs emerged from them. Some were bipedal, some were quadrupedal, and some were "deca-pedal." They just walked around interacting with each other and morphing their forms.

While recording on a camera, The Citizen said, "Amazing! These creatures can freely manipulate their bodies, much like the humble Amoeba. This is amazing. This is wonderful. This is Amazingly Wonderful."

THE MERITORIOUS KNIGHT watched his brother, filled with wonder for these monsters. He pondered to himself if it was a good idea for The Citizen to gain the power of these odd creatures. Before he could ask about this, something spooked the already spooky phantom beasts away. The sphere floated upon the lake. The Citizen, devastated, took the deepest breath of his life and walked out of the bushes. THE MERITORIOUS KNIGHT, in his armor, came out as well. The Ruinous Lady emerged from the top of the sphere.

THE MERITORIOUS KNIGHT uttered, "So, you have revealed yourself."

The Ruinous Lady said, "Rebel in range (Laser Affinity: Causality). Proceeding with the annihilation of rebe...."

After firing a laser at The Ruinous Lady's head, The Citizen said, "Look, I have this day off planned out. Come to this spot, watch some rare creatures, and go back home. Now, I had to deal with this. So, tell me this. Do you call that and (Halberd Proficiency: Existence) this resistiiiinnnngggg!?"

The Citizen chucked his forged weapon at The

Ruinous Lady while she reformed her head. The halberd hit square in the chest, but she seemed unfazed. THE MERITORIOUS KNIGHT was impressed with his brother's uncharacteristic rashness, and he ran at her to attack as well. Before THE MERITORIOUS KNIGHT landed a blow, The Ruinous Lady burst into fragments that fell all over the area.

Still hovering in the air, THE MERITORIOUS KNIGHT exclaimed, "Haha. Nice try, my devoted stalker. That tactical would work on a regular Illecclucian Knight because they need the surroundings to use their technology, but my armor uses actual magic and their technology. So, I am not without multiple options. Give me something new."

The fragments grew into duplicates of her. THE MERITORIOUS KNIGHT just stared down in disbelief. All of The Ruinous Ladies looked up and raised their hands at him. Their palms started to heat up and glow intensely. Then they flung their glowing digits at him, and they exploded on impact. They kept on firing at him while they completely ignored The Citizen. The Citizen ran (Claymore Proficiency: Existence) with his new weapon and cleaved through dozens of them.

Several of them attacked him by wrapping their arms, now turned tendrils around him. The Citizen screamed (Earth Affinity: Causality), "Get Off!!!" Big rocks manifest from his voice, knocking them all off. Some of the remaining Ruinous ladies started shooting at The Citizen. He ducked (Evasiveness: Space) and phased underground to dodge the blasts.

With a powerful glow, THE MERITORIOUS

KNIGHT charged through the blasts and slammed into his attackers, reducing them into puddles. Underneath the last group of duplicates (True Destructiveness: Existence), the ground shook and cracked, revealing rusty brown colored lights. The earth burst wide open, and a powerful explosion struck them all down for good. The Citizen crawled out of the small crater to see his brother, and they bumped elbows at a job prematurely done. From a dark sky, more of the ruinous matter came down by the tons until there was a giant golem in front of them.

The Ruinous Golem roared, "Eliminate Rebel and Ally!"

The Citizen said, "You know what? I'm done with this. I should've done this in the beginning."

THE MERITORIOUS KNIGHT asked, "What?"

The Citizen said, "I send your things to you, bye."

The Citizen pushed (Illecelucuu Affinity: Space) his brother into a rift. The Ruinous Golem stopped and backed off. The Ruinous Lady emerged from her construct. She looked around to find her target but could not find anything. The Citizen tried to shoo her away. She stared at him, went back to the sphere, and it floated away. The Citizen sat on the ground, sighing in relief and frustration with today's events.

The Citizen thought it would take another couple of months to find the phantom beasts again, and he decided to go pack and go home. Standing behind him, those beings glared at him, and he looked back at them. One of them placed its appendage near his eyes. The Citizen guessed what it wanted and took off his contact lens to reveal his actual eyes. The phantom beasts reveal glowing wisps within their bodies.

Before his vision faded, The Citizen said to them, "Hee Hee. You wanted to see my soul before you showed me yours, eh?"

The Citizen spent the rest of the night watching the phantom beasts continue their festivities. He was glad he stuck around instead of teleporting home in a huff. Now, his expedition was complete.

PASSAGE #2: TALES OF THE IVORY ROAMER- PART 4

The Citizen sat with his niece, watching some television until he said it was time for her to go to bed. The Pigtailed Girl did not want to go, and he said he would read her another story about the Ivory Roamer. She still did not want to go. So, The Citizen said he would make it "real-ish," like a movie. The Pigtailed Girl ran (Speed: Space) to her room with The Citizen already there. She went under the blankets, and The Citizen pulled out sheets of paper. He began to read (Storytelling Proficiency: Existence) the first page, and brown energy swirled around them, making the images of what he was about to say:

"Tale of The Ivory Roamer"

Part 4: The Lovely Demons

The Ivory Roamer traversed across the land of light while witnessing the more effects of the gateway remained open. The once white fields are transforming into terrains of twilight as the colors of darkness mix with the world. Eventually, he came across a town and decided to rest before continuing his journey. As he walked through, he saw a lot of children crying. The Ivory Roamer asked one of the children, "What is the matter? Why are all of you crying?" The child said that all of their parents had been taken by demons. They came to their town two days ago in human form with unrivaled beauty. Their mothers, fathers, and even older children soon ran off with them into the middle of the forest. One child tried to stop them, but the winged demons were very fast and almost killed him.

The Ivory Roamer wanted to rest but reluctantly decided to go into the forest to save the adults. The Ivory Roamer wandered through the woods until he reached the center and saw the town's women and girls dancing in one site with the male demon and men with the female one in another location. The Ivory Roamer looked around to see what could be used to fight the monsters. He remembered during his travel that there was a patch of earth that would soon collapse and become a sinkhole. This will not be enough to stop demons who could fly unless they do not have a way to escape. He looked around and found a boulder and managed to lift the large rock with all his might. He transported it to the trap site. Now, it was time to trap those two birds underneath one stone, but first, he returned to town to tell the children that he had a plan to save their parents. The kids rejoiced, and The Ivory Roamer asked the two of the fastest children in this town to help him. Two children stepped forward; one was a boy, and the other was a girl. Ivory Roamer wanted the boy to head for the site where all the women were and attract the male demon. The girl should do the same in the other location. Their job was to lure them to the area where The Ivory Roamer would be waiting. The two children were scared, but they understood why this was important. The Ivory Roamer held out both hands and placed them on top of the children's heads.

It was time to implement Ivory Roamer's plan. He stood and waited at his trap site, waiting for the children. Soon, they had arrived, and The Ivory Roamer told them to hide in the bushes. The demons swooped into the scene swiftly. The Ivory Roamer said to the demons that he was the one who lured them here to defeat them. They ran toward The Ivory Roamer, transforming themselves into monstrous creatures before attacking him. Since they flew, they did not step on the sinkhole spot. So, The Ivory Roamer needed to think creatively. The demons were too fast and knocked him around. The kids jumped out of the bushes and shouted at them. The demons chased them, but that was the moment that The Ivory Roamer needed to grab both monsters' necks and slammed them on top of the intended spot. The impact caused the sinkhole to open up under the demons to fall into. Next, The Ivory Roamer tossed the nearby boulder at the hole covering it. This assured all that the demons could not escape. Later on, the adults returned from the town with no idea of what transpired. The children were happy to see them returned. The Ivory Roamer looked from afar and continued on his quest to return to the gateway.

The End

The Citizen deactivated his power, and The Pigtailed Girl was asleep. He left her room and walked down the hallway, thinking about what would happen later in his story. The Ivory Roamer would be walking towards the sunset and behind him stood a young boy with a brown aura.

PASSAGE #3: THE CHOSEN ONE'S CREW

The Citizen walked down the street, heading to his apartment. He saw many people gathered in front of his home that caught on fire. The Citizen passed the crowd and stared (Water Affinity: Probability) at the sky. The atmosphere turned dark and started to rain heavily. The excessive downpour extinguished the flames, and all the tenants celebrated. They all returned to their homes to check on their possessions. Before The Citizen could go inside his apartment, he was grabbed by massive arms and pulled away to an alley. He tried to struggle (Evas...) free, but he was spritzed with some knock gas and fell asleep.

The Citizen woke up encased in cement. He also felt chains wrapped around him beneath the cold cement. He looked to see where he was, but it was too dark until a light was shining at his face. A young man with a sharp black haircut with a blue streak walked up to The Citizen.

After pulling out a Bo Staff, The young man said, "So, we finally meet. The man who keeps on giving our Chosen One such horrible nightmares."

The Citizen stayed silent.

The young man continued, "I am her right hand. It is her quest to save the world, and you seem to make things more difficult for her and us."

The Citizen remained silent with a smile.

Irritated by The Citizen's response, The Deputy demanded, "I want you to back off, or we will have to make you."

The Citizen remained silent as the ceiling lights turned on to reveal more of The Chosen One's team. The Citizen first noticed The Mutant standing tall, and The Mutant walked toward him, seemingly ready to fight.

The Mutant roared, "We shouldn't be wasting our breath on this guy. He is just like his mother, a demon hiding his true nature."

The next one to walk forward was an automaton with exposed, glowing, blue circuitry, and it said:

"1. I never observed this human before to know what he is capable of.

"2. We must do what we must to protect the chosen human."

"3. 10101011100011110001101010101010."

The Citizen complained, "Great, another man-made thing with a bizarre speech pattern."

Then from another room, The Vagabond, with an antenna- sporting imp holding on to his left arm, said, "He is wily, but nothing too extraordinary. I think that is why she recruited me because I beat this guy one on one."

With nervous fidgeting, The Imp whimpered, "We should just leave this man alone. I don't like the way he is looking at us.

The Citizen asked, "Are you the only ones here?"

The Deputy replied, "Of course, we didn't even tell the boss. We figured it would be a surprise for her to know that you won't be bothering us again."

The Citizen said, "Good (Evasiveness: Space), I didn't want to get into a real fight tonight."

The Citizen phased out of his binds. The Deputy, Vagabond, and Imp gasped. The Mutant snarled, and The Automaton spouted out 1's and 0's. They all attacked (Electricity Affinity: Causality) at once but were blown away by The Citizen's electrical attack, which he fired from his mouth. The crew fell, and The Citizen pulled out his cellphone. He heard footsteps before he could call, and The Chosen One appeared. She was upset because all her friends were hurt. The Vagabond stood up and swung his sword, Firearm Dusk, to release its many shards at The Citizen.

The Vagabond said confidently, "Don't worry. He won't escape this attack."

The Citizen stood (Metal Affinity: Existence) still as shiny, bronze-colored material sprang out and blocked all the shards. Next, it curled up into a ball with all the fragments inside. The Vagabond immediately realized he was out of his league. Behind him, The Citizen smacked the ball right at him, and Chosen One knocked both of them to the ground. The Citizen got to The Chosen One as she tried to crawl away.

As The Citizen grabbed (Mind: Causality) her, He said, "Look, Incomiber, I don't want to sound like a real softy, but I am letting you and your chums go. It is only because you are more valuable free than in a prison cell. I hope you understand what I am saying."

The Citizen did what he needed to do and walked away. The Chosen One felt a bit woozy but managed to get back up and tended to her team. The Citizen hoped what he did worked. He forgot to ask if they were responsible for that fire, and it did not matter right now at this moment. He needed to go back home to see if everything was okay.

PASSAGE #4: THE PROLOGUE OF THE DESTINED BATTLE

Time	The Chosen One	The Citizen	The Dark One
12:00 am	Asleep in a forest where she believes The Dark One would appear.	Sleeping in his apartment.	Basking underneath the moonlight on the balcony of his new hovering fortress.
1:00 am	Asleep	Asleep	Following The Chosen One through his radars and scanners in his mobile fortress.
2:00 am	Asleep	Asleep	Reaching the location where The Chosen One

				was going to hit next.
3:00 am	Asleep	Asleep		Asleep
4:00 am	Asleep	Asleep		Asleep
5:00 am	Asleep	Asleep		Asleep
6:00 am	Asleep	Waking up, took a shower, and watched TV.		Asleep
7:00 am	Asleep	Eating breakfast.		Asleep
8:00 am	Asleep	Walking around the neighborhood.		Waking up and had breakfast in bed.
9:00 am	Asleep	Going to his storage facility to borrow something.		Taking a long herbal bath after a massage.

10:00 am	Asleep	Calling his folks to see what they were up to.	Thinking about how he is going to change the world tomorrow.
11:00 am	Finally, Waking up and ran to the nearest river to bathe.	Watching some videos on the internet.	Reading a book.
12:00 pm	Eating lunch with the crew.	Eating lunch at a burger joint.	Still reading the book.
1:00 pm	Training with her crew to better handle her powers.	Going back home and took a nap.	Eating a fancy meal while looking outside his panoramic window.
2:00 pm	Still training	Asleep	Thinking about how he can defeat his true foe and bring a

			new age to this world.
3:00 pm	Still training	Asleep	Strategizing how he will fight The Chosen One.
4:00 pm	Getting knocked out during training.	Waking up and thinking about what to have for dinner.	Mercilessly beating down several men during his training.
5:00 pm	Unconscious	Cooking steak and fries.	Having another massage.
6:00 pm	Getting up and grabbing some grub with the crew.	Eating dinner.	Having another fancy meal.
7:00 pm	Training once more with her crew.	Getting together with his teammate about their strategy for tomorrow.	Getting dressed by his servants and calling for an assembly.

8:00 pm	Training by herself very intensely.	Finishing with their strategy.	Telling a grand speech about bringing a new way of life for all.
9:00 pm	Training even more because of fear and anxiety.	Going to bed.	Going outside to the balcony, looking at the moon.
10:00 pm	Falling asleep because she trained herself too hard.	Asleep	Going to bed.
11:00 pm	Asleep	Asleep	Asleep
12:00 pm	Asleep	Asleep	Asleep

PASSAGE #5: THE DESTINED BATTLE: CHANGE IS COMING

Wearing black clothing, The Citizen sat in the middle of the woods. He waited for The Chosen and Dark One to get to this location. He turned on his intercom to contact his team.

To The Scholar, The Citizen asked, "What is the situation with those two?"

The Scholar replied, "Both parties have made contact just like we planned. The Dark One is trying to persuade the other to join him, but she isn't budging."

The Heiress chimed in with, "Start Phase 2?"

The Citizen said, "Proceed with Phase 2, and good luck."

After that, The Citizen heard several explosions from a distance. It was time. The Citizen stood up and went to a big machine to turn it on. The Citizen turned (Luck: Space) back around, and two rifts opened up from opposite ends of a small clearing below his spot. The Chosen One came out from one, and The Dark One came out from the other. Both of them were unaware they went through these gateways because they were looking behind them as they were running. Their eyes once again locked with a hint of pure disdain for each other.

The Chosen One spouted, "Should have known you would be one to pull something underhanded like that."

The Dark One rebutted, "I am sorry, using explosives seemed to be your lot's specialty since you blew my old base apart."

The Chosen One said, "I don't know where your old base is, but trust me, if I were there, you wouldn't be here. You would be in a hospital still trying to figure out how you got there. You ****************."

The Citizen, realizing that they will piece together the real culprit, decided to walk out to the clearing to reveal himself. While doing that, small drones flew around the area, showing The President, Vice President, Field Marshall, and other officials what was about to happen. The Citizen strode past the thick trees and made his presence known.

The Citizen said, "Oh, spending too much time with the wrong crowd can give someone such a vulgar vocabulary. Eh, Incomiber."

The Chosen One yelled, "You again."

The Dark One asked, "How did you find us? My mobile base has cloaking technology."

The Citizen said, "Oh, come on, *Stulyranus*. You are supposed to be the smartest of the pair. I only know because I constructed your meet-and-greet."

Both of The Chosen and Dark One said, "What?"

The Citizen continued, "I was the one who was

responsible for attacking your previous base and placed false evidence to frame her. Then I left some clues on where she would turn up next. The challenge was trying to get Incomiber to get here. I "downloaded" this location into her head, making her think it was her idea. It was easier to spoon-feed her the info instead of giving her such a complicated puzzle like yours."

The Chosen One ran at The Citizen because she was enraged by his confession. Before she could land a fist, a giant robot tackled her to the ground. Its arms held her tightly as she kicked and screamed with all her might. Even with her powers, it would not loosen its grip.

The Chosen One screamed, "Ahhhh, What is up with this thing? I crushed this tin can of yours the last time."

The Citizen said, "It is an adapting combat machine that costs a lot of money. You think the government would leave in the dump after one failure. No, they upgraded it, and it learned your fighting style last time. Plus, with all the data that Stulyranus had on you, it is more powerful than ever."

The Dark One bellowed, "You've got my researched data!"

The Citizen responded, "With my lifestyle, I have the keys to any door. Probably should've done more research on the guy who beat you instead of on a gal you never fought before."

The Chosen One uttered, "My friends will get

here and help me beat you and him."

The Citizen said, "I doubt it. I have my own team. One should be entrapping Stulyranus' men with a forcefield and the other dealing with all your crew. Granted, we only came together to stop that man. You are also my target because of your constant meddling in government affairs."

The Dark One turned red as a red ball of energy forged above him. He raised an arm and readied himself to throw at The Citizen. The ball was thrown, but instead of heading for The Citizen, its real target was the robot. The blast blew it apart before it could stab The Chosen One with the needle-like claws. The Citizen was disheartened.

With a chuckle, The Dark One said, "It might have been invincible to her, but it was complete garbage against my power."

The Chosen One survived the explosion angrier than hurt. She walked over to The Dark One and slugged him for doing that before she could escape. The Dark One got up with some blood dripping from his mouth.

The Citizen said, "If that is what you do to your heroes, then I don't want to know what you do to your villains."

After a grunt, The Chosen One said, "You are about to find out."

Once more, The Chosen One ran at The Citizen. She charged up her fist destiny power and threw (Evasiveness: Time) her punch. While she was in slow motion to him, The Citizen moved to the side and set his left leg to trip her. Her attack missed, and she fell hard. The Citizen walked away to go to the robot. The Dark One attempted (Bear Affinity: Existence) to attack him, but a wraithlike bear effigy appeared to pin him down. The Citizen arrived at what was left of the machine. He was upset because his team's whole plan depended on this thing.

The Dark One exclaimed, "What's the matter. Can you continue without your date? If I were you, I would change your strategy."

The Citizen remembered something weeks ago. That dream had to do with that one word. Could change be an existential concept? Might as well try, he guessed. He thought of an attribute that might help in this situation. The bear effigy disappeared so that its conjurer could use a new ability. The Citizen took a breath and invoked the power (Cybernetic Affinity: Change) in his mind.

The Citizen did not notice anything different about him at first. Then he saw his right hand covered with gleaming bronze circuitry. It was only natural with the lack of interest in technology, but it should be enough. He touched his right hand on a small piece of machinery, and the machine reacted and covered it to form a gauntlet. Next, the circuitry grew up The Citizen's arm.

The Citizen grinned at what was happening and chuckled at this very new power. He grabbed many of the robot's parts and placed them on himself. The machinery wrapped his body, making something that would change this fight. As The Fated Ones got back up, they did not see the same enemy they faced before. They saw an armored monster who was laughing maniacally. His helmet covered his face with a robotic eye that glowed brown and locked on to his targets.

PASSAGE #6: THE DESTINED BATTLE: CHANGE IS HERE

As The Citizen walked forward, He said, "Let me ask you a query. Why did I bring all of you to the middle of nowhere? The answer is...So that I can cut loose with no fear of casualties."

The Dark One exclaimed, "I am not your prey. I am your future master."

In a snarky tone, The Citizen demanded, "Then please, my liege, force me to bow."

The Dark One rushed, followed by The Chosen One to attack. The Citizen scanned both of them and used his memory of their fights to calculate a winning strategy. Next, he charged right into The Dark One with his forearm and extended it to push him at The Chosen One. The needles popped out of his gauntlet. The Citizen attempted to stab them, but The Chosen One kicked him in the head, knocking his helmet off. The fated ones stared at him in shock because The Citizen's unique contact lens was knocked off as well. They saw one of his actual eyes, and The Citizen became disoriented by the lack of vision.

The Chosen One uttered, "Wha...What are you? An Alien?"

After retracting his needles, picking up his lens, and inserting it back in, The Citizen said, "My apologies. You shouldn't have seen that."

The Dark One growled, knowing what he might be. He charged up his hand and fired at the ground to create a smokescreen. After the smoke and dust cleared, both fated ones fled. The Citizen got his helmet and preceded to locate them. The Dark One talked to The Chosen One behind a small hill.

The Dark One explained, "This is a horrific predicament. I believe that man is a supernatural creature, a being with a great existential level of power. After my first contact with him, I researched his background, but nothing substantial came up. Now seeing his eye, I remembered seeing a description from a book of mythical organisms about a creature with strange pattern eyes and reality manipulating powers. He must be a Reality- Meister."

Landing in front of them, The Citizen said, "Oh, you read my section. I thought that name was a bit much, but it is accurate. So, you must know my weakness, right?"

The Dark One grunts because he only skimmed through that segment and did not know his weakness. The Citizen laughed and whacked The Chosen One away before she could attack him. He grabbed The Dark One while his enemy struggled to get free but could not.

The Citizen said, "Too bad because it could have turned this battle in your favor. Hakaha."

Then lights glowed above them, and it was The Dark One's mobile fortress. The Chosen One ran up to the distracted Citizen and hit him with a cartoonishly giant bat that sent him flying into the fort. The Dark One stared at The Chosen One angrily, but she smiled patronizingly. He ran and super jumped, using his powers, to his fortress. The Chosen One followed her enemy's lead and super jumped as well.

As soon as The Dark One landed on his fortress, The Citizen grabbed him and waited for The Chosen One to arrive. When she got there, The Chosen One was greeted by The Dark One slamming into her. The Citizen ran off, breaking everything in sight. The Fated Ones were not out and pursued him. Throughout the floating base, The three powerhouses clashed fiercely. With his new computerized mind, The Citizen had the upper hand and simultaneously countered each attack.

Soon, all of them reached the power core of the fort. The Dark One fired an energy blast, but The Citizen punched the attack away. The Chosen One made another giant bat, but The Citizen grabbed the bat this time, and he swung the bat directly at The Dark One.

The Citizen exclaimed, "I am starting to think that I should put an end to all this by taking out this big engine."

The Dark One said, "Then you should get a better look at it."

The Dark One shook the ground by blasting it, throwing The Citizen off balance. The Chosen One dashed in and punched him with enhanced strength right into the power core. The Citizen screamed in pain as pure electricity surged through him. Massive energy waves pushed the fated ones out of the room. The Dark One reached for a nearby intercom to announce to all of his minions to evacuate the fort using the escape pods. The Chosen One ran to the hole that she came in from, and The Dark One pushed her out so that he could escape. Several pods few away from the bastion.

The two landed in the trees and watched the fortress' impending explosion. The mobile base stopped hovering and fell to the ground below, causing the area to shake. The fated ones hit the forest floor because of that shockwave. They were hurting, but they survived the battle with The Citizen. The two got up and stared at each other ready to fight again. Before a single blow was made, the fortress started making loud noises as if there was heavy construction going on in there. The fort's side opened up by a pair of giant, mechanical hands.

The Dark One gritted his teeth, and The Chosen One shuddered at the prospect that The Citizen was not done yet. The President and company watched this development through the drones. The fort split in two to reveal a 20 feet tall mech. Its eyes glowed brown, and then its speakers turned.

The Citizen laughed, "HAHAHAKEKEHAAoOoR!!"

PASSAGE #7: THE DESTINED BATTLE: CHANGE IS HERE TO STAY

The Citizen's laugh was like thunder across the forest. The Chosen One, Dark One, Scholar, Heiress, and everyone else trembled in complete terror. The President looked at The Field Marshal, knowing precisely what was happening. The Citizen had gone manic.

After his laugh, The Citizen shouted, "I never expected to reach this kind of power through one ability! I want to see what this new form can do. In my head, I called my first form my Cybernetic Look and the one after that my Cybernetic Look: Combat Adept Model. So, what should I call this one? Hmmm. I got it. This is my Cybernetic Look: Fortress Suit Model. It's Perfect! Just Perfect! Eeeeeeeekeeeeheeeee!"

The Chosen One's team got to her, and The Citizen reacted by glowing in electrifying, white light. The mech's head opened up, and a cannon was in it, glowing with the same luminosity. The Dark One tried to run, but it was too late.

The Citizen shouted, "NO, INTERLOPERS!!!"

The cannon fired a massive shockwave which engulfed the immediate area in blinding radiance. A few government drones were destroyed in the blast, but The President and other officials could still see the battle. When the light died down, a blue barrier crumbled but not before protecting everyone, even The Dark One. The Chosen One collapsed, and The Mutant ran at The Citizen with anger in his heart. He put all of his abnormal strength in one arm, swung at him but barely made a dent.

The Citizen punched him into the air only to karate chopped him. This sent the poor man straight to the ground with a big "Thud!" The Citizen laughed, and The Automaton shot lasers at him. The Dark One fired some blasts with it, but the assault did not seem to be working. The Citizen retaliated with a red laser flying all over the place.

Everyone frantically ran in circles to evade the beams until they stopped raining down. The Chosen One woke and told her friends to retreat while she would stay here. Her crew refused, and The Dark One stayed, so he reclaimed the mech since it was his fortress once. Before The Citizen continued his onslaught, he heard someone talking on his intercom, and it was The President contacting him.

She said, "Hey, you're wrecking the place with all that firepower."

The Citizen exclaimed, "Oh, don't worry, Pres Sis. You gave me this mission, and I am going to see this through."

The Field Marshal said, "Listen, you need to...."

Before he could hear the rest, The Citizen was struck by the combined force of The Fated Ones. The giant machine fell to the ground on its back. The Dark One fired some cheap shots on the mech's foot to add insult to injury. The Citizen got annoyed, and he slowly started to regain some of his senses. He thought this form was powerful, but it was too much of an easy target. Looking around to see all his destruction, this form may be too powerful. He thought it was time to update.

The Citizen uttered, "Hahahahkehahahaoor, That was a good one, you guys, but I am not done, I am not done, I Am Not Done! It's time for the ULTIMATE ULTRA UPGRADE!"

The top of the mech began to shake and rattle. Nobody knows what was happening this time. A massive chunk of the machine flew off along with the head and began morphing. The chuck broke up into three separate pieces, and they floated right in front of the sun as they took on their final shapes. The parts together resembled The Citizen's mark, but they descended to reveal something more. One of the pieces was a big wheel, another was a long, narrow pyramid, and the last one was a cube.

The Citizen's voice came out from the wheel, and he said, "NoOOoWww, Let's keep this battle between us three, shall we?"

The cube broke up to even smaller ones, 27 to be exact, with a hand on each one. They flew around the group to distract and confuse them until some of them grabbed the crew and took them away. The Chosen One tried to get them back, but a laser was fired near her. It came from the opened tip of the pyramid and extended itself to be more serpentine. The Dark One attempted to shoot it only to be bumped by the wheel. The fated ones were in quite a bind, and it only got worse when tinier cubes returned.

All the cubes converged on The Dark One while The Chosen One fought the wheel and the pyramid. The Dark One was overwhelmed and could not land a single hit on them. Then he felt a staggering amount of pain on his side, and it was one of the cubes with needles protruding from it. He batted it away, but the others hit him even harder to the point that he felt some bones breaking. The Dark One fell over in immense pain, and the cubes flew over to The Chosen One.

The Chosen One was frustrated with the hit-and-run tactics of these two machines until they went away to make way for the cubes. Just like with Dark One, they swarmed around her. The Chosen One made a broad sword and swung it haphazardly, and managed to skewer one. She smiled at this achievement, but it was short-lived when she was stabbed by a cube at the back of her left leg. She kneeled in pain, and the cubes roughed her up but not as bad as The Dark One.

The cubes hovered away and became one again. All of the machines converged, and The Citizen took sighed in relief. He thought this conflict was over, and his sanity almost returned to him. The three pieces floated away from the battlefield, but The Fated Ones stood back up behind them. They limped towards the machines with anguish and determination on their faces.

Getting excited again, The Citizen shouted, "So, obstinate to the very end! Then let's end it!"

The cube split in half, and the wheel came between spinning rapidly, building up electrical energy. The pyramid went to the other machine to feed on the wheel's power. The Citizen would fire one more powerful blast, and The Fated Ones stood their ground. Within a few seconds, the pyramid was fully charged.

The Citizen stated, "You know I was going to let you go off to prison, but now I realize this is no longer a battle of good vs. evil. It is a battle for...."

The pyramid fired a colossal beam as The Citizen screamed, "...CHANGE!" The Chosen One fired blue bullets while The Dark One released a concussive wave of energy. The two attacks combined to form a purple stream of energy. It shredded The Citizen's beam like paper and hit the machines. They began breaking apart for the last time, and the fated ones heard the screams of The Citizen as all the devices got vaporized.

All became silent. The Chosen One was a bit upset that it came down to this. She knew they had their differences, but The Citizen did not deserve that. The Dark One did not care. All he knew was that one big thorn in his side had been plucked out. The fated ones collapsed due to their severe injuries. They could no longer move both their legs because they were broken, and both thought they would just die together. Then The Chosen One's crew returned and got her out of there. They would have tried to finish The Dark One off if his small army did not just arrive simultaneously. In the end, both fated ones made it out of The Citizen's trap, beaten but alive.

PASSAGE #8: EPILOGUE OF THE DESTINED BATTLE

The Heiress and Scholar just arrived on the battlefield between The Fated Ones and The Citizen. No one was left except the giant mech with a gaping hole in its torso. The President started tearing up with her right hand over her eyes, and The Field Marshall kept pounding the table with boiling anger.

The Heiress asked, "Is he really gone?"

Through their intercoms, The Citizen replied, "No, I am always a step ahead of those two."

The Scholar said, "Where are you?"

The Citizen said, "I am in the mech's lower torso. I was simply controlling those machines through my mind. Give me a moment to get out."

The President exclaimed from all their intercoms, "Meeting Room, Now."

The Citizen stood in front of government officials once more, but The Scholar and Heiress were with him this time. The Field Marshall waited in silence, tapping the table. The President and her Vice President soon arrived and sat in the middle of a row of officials. The Citizen asked a nearby secretary to give him an empty cup.

The President spoke, "What has happened

today? I thought you three were to apprehend or neutralize those threats, but instead, I saw long dialogue, an unnecessarily longer fights, and a giant robot which caused more long-lasting harm than good."

"Ma'am, This was more or less our plan from the beginning. You already know I lured both forces to that location to attack them. Yes, arresting them would have been ideal for you all..." The Citizen said, "...but that just won't cut it with these two. We need to monitor them. Let's show them our efforts."

The Scholar uploaded something to the monitors in the room, and they showed a map to the country with two blips on them, one red and one blue. The secretary returned with a cup, The Citizen took (Fruit Punch Affinity: Dimension) it, and a small, red portal opened up. The Citizen scooped up the juice from the gateway and drank it with the cup. The officials were perplexed. So, The Citizen's team explained what happened.

The group stated that they knew that capturing those two would be useless because they would somehow escape captivity. What they needed was a method to watch their every move. The Citizen remembered The Scholar's handy gadget allowed people to see the entire structure of that temple a while back, giving him an idea. He asked his intelligent teammate to make nanobots to keep tabs on them and monitor their health.

It would be no problem to make but how to administer it. The Citizen thought about putting the nanobots into the robot from his old job, and it would inject The Fated Ones with them. With its adaptability and the upgrades The Heiress paid for, he felt it would pose a real challenge for them until they all knew what had happened. That transformation was a last-ditch effort to make the plan work. It was never his plan to be consumed with his new ability, but eventually, he managed to get those cubes to complete the job.

The President said, "Be as it may, You still didn't capture them or eliminate them. They are still out there, and with their injuries, they will be wilier and more desperate. You're temporarily no longer allowed to pursue these individuals and their allies until further notice. I am giving this job to...."

The doors opened wide, and The Zealot in military-style apparel walked in. He stopped right next to the team and saluted all the officials. He turned to The Citizen and gave a smug smile before looking back at The President.

The President continued, "He will be in charge of this mission while you will be head supervisor the excavation sites that your team discovered. You will hand over any information on the threats and your tracking system. Do you, and by extension, your team, accepts this?"

After seeing both teammates nodding, The Citizen replied, "We do."

The President said, "This meeting is adjourned."

PASSAGE #9: AN AWKWARD CHAT

The Citizen and his team left the room. They walked down a hall, discussing what would happen to them. They all agreed that this break was for the best. The Scholar, during the battle, captured his enslaved husband and now was conducting studies on how to cure him of The Dark One's hold. Since she had her husband, The Citizen asked her what would that mean? Would The Scholar permanently leave the team? She said that The Dark One was still out there, and if her friend were ordered to go after him, she would lend her aid. The Heiress thought about going to the islands for a nice, long vacation. The team said goodbye and went their separate ways. Before The Citizen could go back home, The Zealot appeared and got him in a friendly headlock.

The Zealot said, "Hahaha, hey there, heathen."

The Citizen said, "Aemdalis."

The Zealot exclaimed, "Thanks to your ridiculous blunder, I am given the opportunity of a lifetime. It must be eating up inside, knowing that I am going to achieve greatness through the blood and sweat of your labor while you get nothing."

The Citizen said nothing.

After shoving him away, The Zealot said, "Fine,

act mysterious all you like. I am going to catch those two and become famous."

While The Zealot left, The Citizen smiled joyously and said quietly, "Good Luck, Sucker."

The Citizen danced because he had done all his objectives at the end of the day. As a bonus, he was prohibited from searching for The Fated Ones now. The Zealot is going after them, and they will tear him apart. The Citizen could rest and look up high, knowing that this would be a nice change of pace.

The Citizen sat on his couch with his laptop a few days later. He was video chatting with The Zealot about the information about the fated ones. All of the files on them were sent, and before The Zealot could say something awful to him, The Citizen closed his computer. He was glad that was over, and now, it was time for relaxation. The Superhero knocked on the balcony doorway, and The Citizen let him in.

In a somewhat troubled voice, The Superhero asked, "Buddy, have you seen our chosen one? I haven't heard any word from her in days."

The Citizen knew this would happen and made the perfect excuse for this event. The Chosen One and her friends had gone into hiding, and they would not be contacting anyone for a while unless they wanted to face assault squad as guests. Hopefully, they would be caught and put away. So, this excuse would be flawless and would not fail to keep his powerful friend in the dark. The Citizen was going to "I don't know."

The Citizen said, "I...I...I did it."

The Superhero said, "Did what?"

As The Citizen turned away, he said, "I am the reason why she stopped contacting you. I attacked her and The Dark One after luring them to a forest."

In a shocked tone, The Superhero exclaimed. "What?!"

The Citizen continued, "I was simply going to rough her up a bit and let her go. But The Dark One destroyed my robot. So, I had to merge with its parts, become a cyborg, and then lose control of myself. I didn't mean to, and I can't just say this was my job because it never felt right."

The Superhero grabbed The Citizen and said, "You are a fool. Why would you just let this happen?"

Moving free and turning around again, The Citizen spoke, "I never wanted to be part of this conflict. I, of all people, should know how powerful and indomitable metaphysical forces can be. I even told them fighting was useless, but my superiors would not listen. I am telling you all this because you are a man who deserves the truth and not some lazy "I don't know" excuse. If this friendship ends, I want it to end with me coming out with a clean conscience. So, hate if you wish. I..."

The Citizen turned around, and The Superhero was gone. He crawled underneath the blanket of his bed and moaned with such melancholily. The Citizen did not know if his friend forgave him or not for what happened to The Chosen One. The Citizen thought it might be better not to know, or he might get more depressed.

PASSAGE #10: A STROLL AROUND TOWN

Apartment

The Citizen decided to take a long walk around the city to clear his head. He grabbed his coat and locked his door. The old lady with the dogs waved to him down the hallway because her door was opened. Her greeting was silenced by the barking and yelping of her pets. They would jump on him if not for the small plastic gate in front of them. The Citizen waved back and hurried out of there; those dogs annoyed him.

Sidewalk

The streets were buzzing as always, but today feels off. The Citizen lost most of his self-control during the fight with The Fated Ones. The Shrink was going to be furious at him for letting that happen. Especially after The Citizen said that would not occur, he was utterly intoxicated with his new ability, the new possibilities, and the fact that he kept getting stronger. He experienced a lot of joy and excitement, which caused him to go manic, unlike his mother, who goes berserk when argumentative or violent. A mugger waited for anyone to come down to rob in an alleyway. Then a purple glow overcame him, and it slowly glowed blue. The Mugger then ran off somewhere, looking for something.

The Subway Train

The Citizen sat down and watched the train tunnel passing by full of rats, trash, and the occasional homeless. He wondered how The Fated Ones were doing since they were significantly injured. If The Dark One had not destroyed that robot, The Citizen would not have gone down the path to succeeding in his mission. Of course, gaining the power to change would not have happened as well.

The Citizen should have just thought of another way and tested the changing powers later. He was in the midst of battle and remembered that dream, and it was using it now or possibly forgetting it for who knows how long. In hindsight, The Citizen could have just used a syringe and some kind of time manipulation to inject them without them knowing. That is the price of having a nearly endless number of abilities, and one or two of them can be forgotten in the planning stage.

The train reached The Citizen's stop, so he got off. At that time, a quiet businessman with glasses was enveloped in a purple radiance that quickly turned red. The Businessman took off and stepped on his glasses. He ran out of the train with a sinister scowl and bumped past The Citizen. The Citizen did not bother with him, and he continued walking.

The Park

The Citizen walked through a path and enjoyed the unpolluted air. The weather was relatively lukewarm and pleasant. While staring at a lake, he wondered to himself about the choices he made when it came to the fated ones. Maybe The Citizen should have taken that offer The Chosen One gave him. That way, they could have defeated The Dark One and perhaps brought a new age of peace.

Then again, The Chosen One lacked any quality that many great leaders possess, while her counterpart had them in spades. The Dark One must not win either. The Citizen does not like the idea of dealing with an age of tyranny. He should have finished him off when he first met him, but that would mean sacrificing The Scholar and Heiress to do so.

What about the second encounter when he invaded his new base? Maybe, but after hearing his story, The Citizen did not have the heart at that time. Destiny does seem to give those two the means to escape any situation that does not involve another chosen one. All this thinking was stressing him out. He continued through the park to its exit and left.

Tavern

The Citizen was chowing down on a big bowl of fries outside the building. The Mugger just finished running across the city to reach this destination. The Businessman was waiting underneath a lamp post and began to laugh maniacally. The two's eyes were locked, and the air was filled with intensity.

The Businessman uttered, "So, you have come. I don't know why, but I must kill you. Then I will rule the world."

With conviction, The Mugger exclaimed, "I don't

know why either. I was just planning to mug some poor sucker until I felt a new purpose. Then something led me to you."

The Businessman said, "Enough of your crud, just die already."

The Businessman and Mugger ran towards each other while they glowed red and blue, respectively. They pulled back their fists and got ready to strike down their enemy. The two men yelled at the top of their lungs and threw their punches. The two men punched each other right in the face. The Businessman and Mugger fell over and passed out while their colorful auras turned purple and faded away completely. All this happened while The Citizen was not looking.

The Citizen finished and left the tavern while paramedics and cops tended to the two men who had little to no memories of what happened to them. He looked at the situation for a second and decided to go home. It was time to move forward. All this destiny nonsense was over for now. It was time to go back to living again, and The Citizen knew (Avian Affinity: Change) how to start.

The Citizen sprouted brown, luminescent wings. His fingernails were coated with an unearthly, glowing material and pointed outward to resemble talons. That same material covered his mouth to make a beak, but it went away because The Citizen did not like it. After the transformation, he flew up to the sky. The Citizen was screaming with excitement and terror, but mostly excitement. He soared across the city and landed on the roof of his apartment to watch some tv. Across the country, a man was sleeping in his bed until a purple glow overtook him, and he woke up smiling evilly as the aura turned crimson red.

The End of Volume 5

The End of The Ridificci Collection

ACKNOWLEDGEMENT

Proofreaders:

1) B. Liken
2) C. Edwards Johnson
3) W. Wakins
4) C. Drummer

Illustrators:

1) raiyanovi (Fiverr) for Rough Draft of Cover
2) warnakomiks (Fiverr) for Final Draft of Cover/ Concept Art

CONTACT

Go to The Good Enough Evil Page on Facebook for Q&As, updates and more.

Made in the USA
Columbia, SC
30 August 2023